Jesse Ball

The Way Through Doors

Jesse Ball (1978–) is an American poet and novelist. He is the author of *Samedi the Deafness,* published last year by Vintage Books and shortlisted for the 2007 *Believer* Book Award. His first volume, *March Book,* appeared in 2004, followed by *Vera & Linus* (2006), and *Parables and Lies* (2008). His drawings were published in 2006 in Iceland in the volume *Og svo kom nóttin.* He won the Plimpton Prize in 2008 for his novella, *The Early Deaths of Lubeck, Brennan, Harp & Carr.* His verse appeared in *The Best American Poetry 2006.* He is an assistant professor at the School of the Art Institute of Chicago.

Also by Jesse Ball

Samedi the Deafness

The Way Through Doors

Jesse Ball

VINTAGE CONTEMPORARIES

Vintage Books

A Division of Random House, Inc.

New York

A VINTAGE CONTEMPORARIES ORIGINAL, FEBRUARY 2009

Library of Congress Cataloging-in-Publication Data
Ball, Jesse, 1978–
The way through doors : a novel by Jesse Ball.
p. cm.
ISBN 978-0-307-38746-2
1. Psychological fiction. I. Title.
PS3602.A596W39 2009
813'6—dc22
2008022852

Book design by Rebecca Aidlin

Printed in the United States of America
10 9 8 7 6 5 4 3 2

For Catherine Ball

and it doesn't matter, it doesn't mean what we think it does

for we two will never lie there

we shall not be there when death reaches out his sparkling hands

—Kenneth Patchen, "And What with the Blunders"

The Way Through Doors

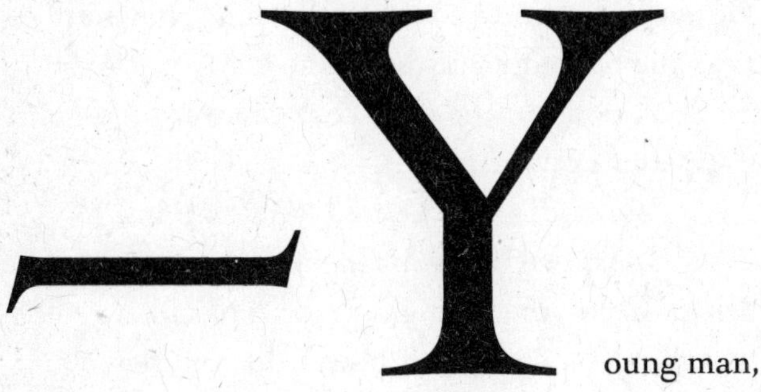

oung man,

let me look at you.

The room was broad, and lit from behind by massive windows that lined the dark mahogany-paneled wall. Light came through in a vague haze, sifted just beyond the glass by the leaves of the oaks from the street. A large man, my uncle, came around the desk towards me.

I, smiling, nodding, trying to look agreeable. My uncle fatter than he had been. But happy. Fat and happy. That's the way. An important man in the governing of the city, my uncle had always been far too busy to bother with such as me.

—My boy, you seem well. Not too long, coming down here on the train? There was an accident just yesterday. Someone got pushed.

5 The way he said it made it sound like the city was a sort of theatrical production.

—Not long, I said quietly. I had my book.

I held up a book. It was a book of letters that desperate Russian poets had sent to an old German poet and he to them during a summer near the beginning of the century. My uncle did not look down at the book, but came around it and slapped me on the back.

—Good, good, he said. (An embrace.)

—You've had your hair cut, haven't you? he asked. Cut with a straight razor, looks like.

10 —Yes, I said, just now. I do it myself, a couple times a year.

—You use a mirror? he asked.

—No, I said, just a razor and a comb. In fact, I close my eyes.

—Not bad, he said. It's the old way, isn't it? Way they used to do it . . . I'd like to see that. Tell me next time, and I'll send the car.

He gave me another pat, then unhanded me, went back around the desk, and sat down with the air of a man who has often sat down in the presence of others who remain standing.

—I have given your situation some thought, 15
Selah. I understand there was this business in C., and I know it distracted you for a while, but god damn it, man, you've got to get yourself together. These scraps of paper . . .

He held up several of my pamphlets. I sat up straight.

—It just won't do you any good. No conceivable good.

—I . . .

—Enough of that, he said. I have conferred with some old friends and I am going to install you in a position of which I feel you are certainly capable. There is a man I know, Levkin. He's an odd man, but trustworthy. I think you can gain much from his acquaintance.

He pressed a button behind his desk, and a 20
door on the far side of the room opened. A man came out. He had evidently been waiting there some time, but he gave no sign of it. Nodding to my uncle, he immediately addressed me.

—Selah Morse?

I nodded. A strange-looking man. He was the sort you could never recall anything about afterwards. Featureless. Not that he didn't have features. He was of a certain height, of a certain weight, etc., but they didn't add up to anything. He was more of an average weight, an average height. If he left the room, who would remember him?

—This way, please.

He looked at me as I stood there, book in hand.

25 My uncle nodded.

—I think you'll find the work pleasant. Come see me in a week or so. We'll lunch together. I know a place. . . .

But already I was following the featureless man through the paneling and down a set of stairs.

At the bottom of the stairs there was a passage that let out onto the street. I tried to place it in my memory in case I ever needed to get up to my uncle's office on the quick. In my head I imagined an enormous house, a mansion I had visited once as a boy. I walked in the front door, along the central hallway. On the right was a room made expressly for telephoning. I entered it, pulled tight the door. Beside the telephone on the nightstand, I placed the idea of this secret entranceway to my uncle's office. Quietly then I exit first the telephone-room, then the mansion, shutting carefully the doors.

—Call me Levkin, the man said shortly.

30 I nodded. There was no need to say my name.

I followed Levkin down the block. He had a rapid way of walking with hardly any wasted motion. He turned several times, finally coming to a sort of pocket-park. In the center, a building. We crossed the park, mounted the steps, and entered, he turning in the lock a sort of monkey-faced key.

Within there was a large room. A desk stood opposite the door. On it a girl lay sleeping. She was quite slender, and expensively dressed.

She gave one the impression of a cat, insomuch as were one to wake her it seemed she would only stalk off to some other equally unlikely napping place, there to resume her slumber.

I looked at Levkin. He had his finger over his lips. Softly he said:

—That's Rita, the message-girl.

—Messages for what? I whispered. 35

—The Seventh Ministry. Municipal Inspection.

He passed on through a left-hand door into a long sort of sitting room. There were tables, chairs, and sofas, as well as a large armoire. He opened it. Inside were a great number of identical suits in various sizes. Identical to the suit he himself was wearing. It was an elegant suit, obviously costly, but very quiet.

—Size? he said.

I reached past him and took the appropriate suit.

—Your office is this way, he said. 40

We exited the sitting room and proceeded back past Rita, who was now awake and watching us with one of two eyes. I said nothing; she said nothing.

—In here, said Levkin.

Through the right-hand door we went. A hallway led to the back of the house. There was a ladder on one side and a stair on the other. Levkin climbed up the ladder. I followed. At the top, a landing and a door. He opened the door.

—Your office. On the desk, a letter in explanation. Rita may or may not be up soon with your tea.

45 Levkin did a sort of half bow, and vanished back through the door and down the ladder, leaving me to survey my new premises. It was a fine room. A very long window ran much of the way along the wall, giving a view out onto the park. A dog was chasing another dog, which was chasing the first dog unsuccessfully. I felt that this meant something. I wrote it down on a pad of paper.

Dog chasing dog itself chasing dog, but not fast enough.

I illustrated the note, took a tack, and pinned it to the wall beside my desk. As I did this, Rita entered and leaned against the wall.

—Dressing up the place? she asked.

—Is that my tea? I asked.

50 —It can be.

She crossed the room and set the tea down on a small table by the window. With a sigh she threw herself down into a large leather chair and sat watching me.

I shook my head. I picked the suit up, went into the bathroom, and changed into it, slowly and carefully. The experience was enormously pleasing. Never had I been in possession of such a fine suit. It fit perfectly. Pants, shirt, vest. There was even a pocket watch.

Rita entered the room.

—Not bad, she said, and held the suit coat up for me.

I slid it on.

—Milk and sugar, I said. Or, just honey. If you're going to do something, you might as well . . .

—I'll write that down somewhere and lose it, she said. The suit fits. Not bad. I imagine you don't know a thing about what goes on here, do you?

—I know enough, I retorted.

—We'll see, she said. If you know anything at all, then why do we keep all our clocks three hours ahead?

We went out into the main room. Sure enough, the clock was three hours ahead.

—Well, that's obvious enough, I said. But I'm busy. Don't you have something to do?

—Try figuring out why you have . . .

She reached into the sleeve of my suit and pulled a long white handkerchief out of a secret pocket. It was monogrammed: *S. M.*

—. . . secret pockets in your clothing. Tell me that, buster.

She spun around and left out a different door, one on the far side of the room.

Only after she was gone did I wonder, how had she climbed the ladder with a cup of tea on a saucer? Evidently there was more to Rita than met the eye, though what met the eye was just fine.

Turning back to the desk I found an envelope. Within there was a letter, two days old.

Seventh Ministry

21 July xxxx

Mr. Selah Morse,

Imagine that you are being written to from a place no larger than a gourd. In this gourd, furthermore, the necessary supplies for writing letters do not exist. Therefore, we make do with other mediums. Or perhaps this business of the gourd is a lie, a simple way of beginning a letter that I had hoped I would never have to write. The simple matter is this—up until now there has always been one Municipal Inspector in the city. For there to be two, well, I simply was not prepared for the circumstance to arise. Yet here you are.

I have it on good authority from Rita, the message-girl, that you cannot be trusted with any task, and that we should despair of your ever becoming a useful member of our little cadre. However, at the time of her saying this, Rita was operating under the clever assumption that you were only an idea and not an actual person. The contrary, rather, is the case. You are an actual person, and the work that you have to accomplish here is merely an idea.

Do you understand? We inspect things. We go about the city and occasionally stir ourselves to inspect virtually anything we choose. Our authority is both unlimited and nonexistent. It operates on a case-by-case basis. On a given day I might have the power to shut down a dam.

The next I cannot cause a street vendor to move from off a corner. Vaguer and vaguer! I'm sure you understand now. After all, you were recommended to us as a sly young man. This you had best prove.

Senior Inspector, Seventh Ministry

Mars Levkin

I set the paper down. By the window I found my tea. It was quite cold. In fact, it looked like someone had been ashing a cigarette in it.

—That wasn't for you to drink, said Rita, opening the door again.

She had a tray this time. On the tray was another envelope, and a cup of tea. She brought it over and set it down gently.

—I'm Rita the message-girl, she said.

—I've been told that, I replied.

She adjusted the hem of her skirt.

—Any messages to send? she said.

—Could you tell Levkin that—

—No! she said. Only written messages. What sort of message girl do you think I am?

She stalked off, leaving me with the tea and letter.

I took a sip of the tea. Irish Breakfast, with just the right amount of milk and sugar. Thank you, Rita. I opened the letter.

Seventh Ministry

21 July xxxx

M.I. Selah Morse,

I do hope you're settling in. Things have been dreadfully strange around here ever since Maude ran away (the gray tabby). I think you are quite handsome and pleasant to talk to, and you mustn't get the wrong idea about me. I am excited to see if you can do the work, and if you like it. Also, I had a cousin named Selah who died when he was very young. He died right after he learned to read. The doctor said some people aren't meant to read. No one knows if he was joking or not, but we have to assume so. Was it a funny joke? I have never been in a position to tell. Anyway, good-bye for now,

Rita Liszt, M.G.

Seventh Ministry

I closed the letter and smiled to myself. On an ordinary day, I would be reading in the park or working on one of my pamphlets in my cramped apartment. Was it true? Had I really come up in the world? I inspected my clothing for secret pockets and found several more, including a rather clever one that went all the way down the pant leg, starting beneath a false belt loop. Or, I suppose, the belt loop was a belt loop truthfully. But it also had this other business of being the start of a secret pocket.

HOWEVER, the true business began later, and about that we will now speak.

Several months, perhaps six or nine, had
passed since I had begun work as an inspector. I was quite used to my schedule and to my responsibilities. It was late in the day, when afternoon has begun quite visibly to crumple around the edges and one can smell rather than sense that evening will soon be upon us. Quite the opposite is true in winter, when one sees night approaching from afar on spindly noiseless legs. But now it was the spring, and I was heading towards a noodle shop happily situated between a sort of pretend-dadaist gallery and an old movie theater named the Grand Corazon. Whenever I was in that neighborhood I made a point of stopping by the noodle shop.

As I walked, a girl came out of a doorway ahead of me and paused in the street. She was very happy, perhaps as happy as a person could be; one could tell this at a glance. She looked up at the second-story window. It was closed. Presumably she had just come from the apartment to which it belonged. The girl was quite fine-looking, with bare shoulders and a beauty that I have always ascribed to the Han dynasty of ancient

China. Not that she was Chinese. No, I didn't know what she was, Slavic maybe, and elegant.

Out of nowhere, a taxi came speeding. There was a great honking of horns, a shouting. The girl made as though to jump back onto the curb, but instead went the other way, out into the street. With a dreadful thud, the braking taxi smashed full into the girl, sending her flying up into the air to land flat on the pavement some twenty feet away. The whole thing was rather like a geometry problem. Except that one could see immediately how truly injured the girl was, and one oughtn't to say such things or even think them at such times.

I dropped the brown paper parcel I was carrying and ran to where she lay. One isn't supposed to lift or move people who have been struck by dynamically heavy and fast-moving objects; however, I couldn't help but lift the girl off the street. She was completely unconscious. All her gladness had paused a moment.

—Driver! I shouted.

The cabdriver approached reluctantly, looking away and mumbling things to himself. I could see he would be of little use in the fast-approaching solution. Nevertheless,

—Driver!

—Sir, and —I didn't see her, and —She came out of nowhere.

—We must get this girl to the hospital. Pull the cab up here.

In moments the cabdriver had pulled the

cab up beside the struck girl. We lifted her into the back of the taxi. I climbed in the front with the driver. Away we went.

+ + +

An orderly came and took the unconscious girl away down the hall on a gurney, leaving me standing before the emergency desk. I started to go after, but the clerk called out to me.

—What's her name? You have these forms to fill out.

—I don't know, I said.

—But you *are* the one who brought her in, no?

—Yes, but I don't know her. I only saw the accident.

—All right, well, do you think she would want you to stay with her?

—I suppose so, I said. If I were in an accident, I would want someone to stay with me.

—Me too, said the clerk.

—All right, I'll go down there then.

—Third room on the left, he said, and gave me an approving nod.

These sorts of nods, from complete strangers during trying circumstances, help to cement one's self-worth in a way that a compliment from a friend never can. All-embracing, they confer a general air of approval upon one's movements for a brief time. No price can be put on them.

The third room on the left was not really a room. It was just a screened-off area of a big room. The girl lay, still unconscious, breathing softly. The orderly looked up when I came in.

—Are you her boyfriend?

—Yes, I said.

—What's her name?

—Mora Klein.

The orderly wrote that down.

—And your name? he asked.

—Selah Morse.

—You know, she doesn't have any identification on her.

—I'm aware of that, I said. She doesn't like to carry identification. She never wants anyone to know who she is.

—Inconvenient, isn't it? asked the orderly.

—You have no idea, I said. When will she come out of it?

—Any minute, he said. I gave her a shot.

—What kind of shot? I asked.

—Just a shot, he said.

And just at that moment, she began to stir. Her eyes opened and she looked dazedly around. She started to sit up, but the orderly held her down.

—Where am I? she asked.

Her voice was very fitting. It sounded like the comforting noises that faraway things make in morning.

—Mora, you're in the hospital, I said. You were in an accident.

—It'll be all right, the orderly told her. Your 125
boyfriend's here. He brought you.

—Yes, I said, I'm here.

She looked at me, smiled, and closed her eyes.

—Stay here, said the orderly. Keep talking to her. Try to keep her awake. The doctor will be here in a moment.

I looked down at Mora. Her face was a bit pale, but she seemed remarkably unhurt. I didn't see any bruises or lacerations on her face, arms, or hands. She must have landed entirely on her head.

—You've got to stay awake now, Mora. The 130
hospital doesn't want you to fall asleep. If you do, you'll sleep forever, and that wouldn't be any good for any of us.

Mora opened her eyes again. They were gray. She looked up at me.

—Who are you? she asked.

—Selah Morse, I said again. You don't remember me?

—No, she said. I don't remember anything.

—Well, don't worry, I said. Things will be 135
sorted out shortly. The important thing is that you're okay.

She smiled again and closed her eyes. The doctor came in.

—Mr. Morse? he asked.

I did a half bow.

—I'm Dr. Platt. You'll have to leave while we examine the patient. Someone will fetch you afterwards.

140 —Good-bye for now, Mora, I said, bending over the gurney and kissing her on the cheek.

I wasn't sure whether I was going to do it, and then I had done it. Her skin was very soft.

—Good-bye, she said.

+ + +

After fifteen minutes or so, an attendant came out to call me back in. He was a large man, quite hairy.

—Morse! he called out.

145 —Here, I said, and hurried after.

As we walked down the hall, the doctor emerged from a side room.

—Well, he said, she had quite a blow to the head. Strangely, her body is largely unhurt where the taxi hit her. The only damage is due to the concussion. She seems to have entirely lost her memory. It will come back, probably, but these things take time. It would be helpful for you to construct a book for her, detailing her past circumstances. Such memory aids can help patients regain what they've lost.

—I see, I said.

—The important thing for the next eighteen hours, he said, is to keep her awake. She can be discharged tonight, as long as you'll take her somewhere quiet and stay with her.

150 —I'll do that, I said.

We had paused in the hall. The hairy attendant had gone on. The doctor's expression was kind. He gave the impression of being in the process of doing a hundred things at once, yet having truly and certainly a moment free in which to stand here quietly speaking with me.

—I'll do that, I said again.

—Good, good. There'll be some papers to sign. Insurance, etc. You should go in now and see her. She's been asking for you.

I shook his hand.

—Thanks, Dr. Platt, I said.

—No trouble.

The doctor paused a moment longer. He looked on the verge of asking me a question.

—If you don't mind my asking, he said, where do you buy your suits?

I looked at him a moment.

—It's just that they remind me of the sort the secret policemen used to wear back in Albania. I was raised there. I'm sure it's the same design.

I held out my arm for him to feel the fabric. He did.

—From an Albanian tailor on East Fourth Street, I said.

I considered telling him about the secret pockets, but refrained.

—The man's a miscreant, I continued. He is difficult to deal with. The only way we can get him to do anything is by sending a girl named Rita over. She's lovely and young, and he'll talk to her.

165 —Thanks, said Dr. Platt. I'll look into it. East Fourth . . .

—Between First and Second, I finished.

—You make that book for her, he said. Everything you can remember about her life. No matter how small or picayune.

—I'm looking forward to it, I said.

+ + +

I went back into Mora's room. She was wearing a hospital gown, sitting up, and eating what looked like a bowl of vanilla ice cream.

170 —I thought that was reserved for children who've just had their tonsils out, I said reprovingly.

—Didn't I get my tonsils out? she asked, as if meanwhile winking, though she did not actually wink.

This was a special gesture that she had perfected.

—Not yet, I said. We can stay for that, though, if you like.

—I'd rather go, she said. Can we?

175 —Yes, let's, I said. Give me a moment.

I went back out into the hall and down to the clerks' counter. I showed them my Seventh Ministry badge and explained that this visit had never taken place. While there was no real reason for them to believe me, they did. Through a half-open door, the doctor was watching me. I smiled and waved. He waved back. I returned to Mora's room.

—Well, Mora, I said. It's time to go. Get changed and we'll head out.

—To where? she asked.

—Well, I suppose we'll go back to my place.

—All right, she said. Close that curtain and help me with this thing.

I shut the curtain and turned around. She had gotten out of bed and was trying unsuccessfully to untie the dressing gown. She turned her back to me.

—Untie that, she said. You know, this is all very strange. I don't remember you at all. Not even a little. Are you sure you're my boyfriend?

—Quite sure, I said. You have a little tattoo of the Morton salt girl with an umbrella on the small of your back.

—Do I? she asked, trying to look over her shoulder.

—No, I said. I was just joking.

I untied the dressing gown. Underneath she had only her underwear on, and it was all I could do to act as though I had seen this spectacle a thousand times. I fetched her dress from off a chair and handed it to her. She pulled it over her head, then slipped on a pair of green shoes. Extending her arm, she said:

—Shall we?

—Yes, let's.

And so we left the hospital together. There was a line of taxis outside. I chose one at random and told the cabbie my address. Mora sat down in the taxi and I sat beside her.

190 —I'm not entirely sure, she said, that I ever knew you.

—Be sure of it, I said. You've got to stay awake.

—How will I manage it? she asked. I'm already tired.

—Easy enough, I said. I'll tell you stories.

—That sounds just fine, said Mora, resting her head on my shoulder. When will you begin?

195 —At the room I let, I said. Many things begin there.

+ + +

My apartment was in the top floor of an old building. It had an elevator controlled by cables, and wide factory windows. Mora was pleased greatly by the elevator, and even more so by my rooms. I had purchased an old printing press with the money I made from my new profession, and I had outfitted the place as a thoroughgoing pamphleteer's hideout.

She sat down on a sofa and looked around happily.

—Something to drink? I asked.

—A mint julep, she said. That and only that.

200 Luckily I was in the habit of drinking mint juleps. I made a pitcher and brought it in. The making of mint juleps is a glad and pleasing experience, particularly when it is done on the behalf of a young woman who has lost her memory.

—And now, I said, handing her a tumbler full of ice, our story begins.

I took a long drink of mint julep.

—Young man, let me look at you.

The room was broad, and lit from behind by many tiny windows that lined the stark white walls. Light came through in a hideous clarity, focused just beyond the glass by the shining leaves of the enormous oaks from the street. A thin man, my uncle, came around the desk towards me.

I, smiling, nodding. My uncle looked very glad to see me. Always pleasant to be seen by one who's glad to see you. That's the way.

—My boy, I heard the bad news. If there's anything I can do for you . . . I hope the car ride wasn't too long. I told them to come directly, of course.

—Not long. I had a newspaper.

—Good, good. (An embrace.)

—You've had your hair cut, haven't you? he asked. Cut with a straight razor, looks like.

—Yes, I said, just now. I do it myself, a couple times a year.

—You use a mirror? he asked.

—No, I said, just a razor and a comb. In fact, I close my eyes.

—Not bad, he said. It's the old way, isn't it? Way they used to do it . . . I'd like to see that. Tell me next time, and I'll send the car. Anyway, you might want to use a mirror. You missed a few spots.

He gave me another pat, then unhanded me, went back around the desk, and sat down with the air of a man who has often sat down in the presence of others who remain standing.

—I have given your situation some thought, Selah. It has come to my attention that you could use a bit of work. I thought about several of the many options that exist and I have come to certain conclusions.

—I . . .

—Enough of that, he said. I have conferred with some cronies of mine, and I am going to install you in a position, the duties of which I'm certain you will discharge.

He pressed a button behind his desk and a door on the far side of the room opened. A man came out. He seemed to be in a hurry. Nodding to my uncle, he immediately addressed me.

—Selah Morse?

I nodded. A strange-looking man. He reminded me of a devil-bird that once had roosted in the tree outside of my window. It would never leave, but would always sit upon a certain branch and cackle at me. Whenever it was present, I would have bad dreams. I passed two years of my life in this way with the devil-bird.

—Come with me please.

He watched me as I stood there.

My uncle nodded.

—I think you'll find the work fascinating. Come and see me sometime. We'll go to the zoo after hours and shoot ducks.

But already I was following the birdlike man through the paneling. There was a chute there. I climbed into it and found myself shot out of a vent unit onto a grassy lawn at street level.

—Call me Levkin, the man said in a very comforting voice.

I nodded.

I followed Levkin down the block. He had a rapid way of walking with hardly any wasted motion. He turned several times, finally coming to a sort of pocket-park. In the center, a grand building in the Federalist style. We crossed the park, mounted the steps, and entered, he turning in the lock a sort of monkey-faced key.

Within there was an entry room. A desk stood opposite the door. On it a very pretty girl lay sleeping. She was quite slender, and expensively dressed. She gave one the impression of a cat, insomuch as were one to wake her it seemed she would be likely to scratch or bite you with great animosity.

I looked at Levkin. He had his finger over his lips. 230
Softly he said:

—That's Rita, the message-girl.

—Messages for what? I whispered.

—Just to keep us on our toes, you know, he whispered back.

He passed on through a left-hand door into a long sort of sitting room. There were tables, chairs, and sofas, as well as a large armoire. He opened it with the same monkey-faced key. Inside were a great number of identical suits, in various sizes. Identical to the suit he himself was wearing. It was an elegant suit, obviously costly, but very quiet. As quiet as the passage of six mice over a carpet.

—Is it always that quiet? I asked. 235

—Generally, he said. What's your size?

I reached past him and took a suit at random.

—Your lair is up a ladder, he said.

I grinned. What a fine fellow Levkin was turning out to be.

We exited the sitting room and proceeded back past 240
Rita, who was still quite asleep. From this new angle I could partially see down the front of her shirt. It was very exciting.

—In here, said Levkin.

Through the right-hand door we went. A hallway led to the back of the house. There was a ladder on one side and a stair on the other. Levkin climbed up the ladder. I followed. At the top, a landing and a door. On the door there was a nameplate. It said, SELAH MORSE, MUNICIPAL INSPECTOR. He opened the door.

—Your office. On the desk, a letter in explanation. Rita will follow, perhaps bringing tea. She is difficult to predict.

Levkin did a sort of half bow, and vanished back through the door and down the ladder, leaving me to survey my new premises. It was a fine room. A very long window ran much of the way along the wall, giving a view out onto the park. A dog was chasing another dog, which was chasing the first dog unsuccessfully. I felt that this meant something. I wrote it down on a pad of paper.

Dog chasing dog itself chasing dog, but not fast enough.

I illustrated the note, took out a penknife, held the note against the wall, and stabbed the penknife through it. I checked. The note was held securely. As I did this, Rita entered and leaned against the wall.

—Dressing up the place? she asked.

—Is that my tea? I asked.

—It can be.

She crossed the room and set the tea down on a small table by the window. With a sigh she threw herself down into a large leather divan and sat watching me.

I shook my head. I picked the suit up, went into the bathroom, and put it on. It fit perfectly. Pants, shirt, vest. There was even a pocket watch. My old clothes I put into a chute labeled,

THE FIRE THAT AWAITS US

Rita came into the bathroom.

—Not bad, she said, and held the suit coat up for me.

She spun around and left out a different door, one on the far side of the room.

Only after she was gone did I wonder, how had she climbed the ladder with a cup of tea on a saucer?

Turning back to the desk I found an envelope. Within there was a letter, three days old.

Seventh Ministry

20 July xxxx
Mr. Selah Morse,

I have it on good authority from Rita, the message-girl, that you cannot be trusted with any task, and that we should despair of your ever becoming a useful member of our little cadre. However, at the time of her saying this, Rita was operating under the clever assumption that you were only an idea and not an actual person. The contrary, rather, is the case. You are an actual person, and the work that you have to accomplish here is merely an idea.

An elephant wandered apart from Hannibal's army as he was crossing the Alps. It ventured into a Swiss town and befriended a man named Tulich. Tulich went on to become the greatest clockmaker the world has ever seen, mostly, we now think, because of the secrets the elephant told him.

Do you understand? We inspect things. Vaguer and
vaguer! I'm sure you understand now. After all, you were recommended to us as a sly young man. This you had best prove.

Senior Inspector, Seventh Ministry

Mars Levkin

I set the paper down. By the window I found my tea. It was quite warm still. The appropriate amount of milk and sugar was in it.

—Don't drink too much, said Rita, opening the door again. It's poisoned. Only slightly, but still poisoned. I had decided to poison you and give you the antidote every day so that you would be forced to obey me, but now I've changed my mind.

She had a tray this time. On the tray was another envelope, and a cup of tea. She brought it over and set it down gently.

—I'm Rita the message-girl, she said.

—I've been told that, I replied.

She adjusted the hem of her skirt.

—Any messages to send? she said.

—Could you tell Levkin that—

—No! she said. Only written messages. Or phone messages. What sort of message girl do you think I am?

She stalked off, leaving me with the tea and letter.

I took a sip of the tea. Earl Grey, with just the right amount of milk and sugar. Thank you, Rita. I opened the letter.

Seventh Ministry

20st July xxxx
M.I. Selah Morse,

I do hope you're settling in. Things have been dreadfully strange around here ever since Maude ran away (the gray tabby with the cute limp). I think you are quite handsome and pleasant to talk to, and you mustn't get the wrong idea about me. I am excited to see if you can do the work, and if you like it. Also, I had a cousin named Selah who died when he was very young. He died right after he learned to read. The doctor said some people aren't meant to read. Giving him a book, say, *Goodnight, Moon,* was as good as murder. No one knows if he was joking or not, but we have to assume so. Was it a funny joke? I have never been in a position to tell. Anyway, good-bye for now.

Rita Liszt, M.G.

Seventh Ministry

I closed the letter and smiled to myself. On an ordinary day, I would be reading in the park or working on one of my pamphlets in my cramped apartment. Was it true? Had I really come up in the world?

I went back into the bathroom and examined myself in the mirror. The suit did fit rather well. This was the first *uniform* I had ever worn, and it was pleasing to me in some sense to be a part of a larger endeavor. When I came out of the bathroom, Levkin was seated by the window.

—Can't stay in one place, can you? I said.

—Mostly, he said. Anyway, that's the job. Do you understand what's involved?

—When do we leave? I asked.

—Let me tell you a story, he said. By way of illustrating a point. There was a man named Carlov. He was a strongman in a circus. His trick—you know, all performers have to have some trick—was to pick himself up. Now most people, no matter how strong they are, cannot pick themselves up. Somehow Carlov was able to do this, I guess it was a matter of leverage or something. You know, where his muscles were connected, etc. In any case, he would come out onstage, pick himself up, stand there for a while, while everyone gawked—I mean, the thing looked totally impossible—and then put himself back down. He made loads of money, but most of it went to his manager, a guy named Wales Carson. In the end, I was asked by the city to investigate these proceedings. I went down there and watched the performance for days. I went dozens of times. I just couldn't figure out how he was managing to pick himself up.

Levkin took a pack of cigarettes out of his pocket, lit one, and leaned back in his chair.

280 —So what happened? I asked. How was he doing it?

—No one knows, said Levkin. Two days later he got pushed out a window on Fortieth and Third Avenue.

He took another puff of his cigarette.

—The point is, don't work too hard. Most things solve themselves. However, it is important for us to be mixed-up in things. You understand.

I said that I most certainly understood and that definitely we were all going to get on well together.

285 —Good, he said.

And so my time at the Seventh Ministry began. At first I accompanied Levkin on inspections. We burst into a tax office off Varick Street, demanding that all documents pertaining to the twelfth of February, 1995, be summarily destroyed. We watched over this destruction with a baleful eye, and forced the supervisor to sign a form agreeing that we had never been there. This form we posted on his office wall. Later that day we visited the police horse stables below Canal and spent a while feeding the horses carrots and cubes of sugar.

Slowly, I began to understand what was expected of me. We were a randomizing element in the psychology of the city. We were the practical element of the philosophy that all parts in a system should not react the same way. As you may expect, this was enormously pleasing to me. I had never expected that my uncle, a man of sober resolution, could ever countenance such behavior. And yet he knew of it. In part it was his power, the power of men like him, that helped to lend the Ministry its dubious clout. All along I must have misjudged the man. Of course, I would never tell him. If he did in fact deserve this new standing in my esteem, then telling him would be pointless. He would already know.

Soon things started settling into a routine. I moved into a better apartment with the better money I was making, a place closer to the Ministry. I was provided with many iterations of my suit, the which I kept in a large wardrobe. I began to feel confident about my work, and went around on my own, inspecting and interrogating. I found that the authority of the badge was virtually unlimited. Even the police force seemed to be a bit in awe of it. There was a number on the badge, and when they ran it in their squad-car computers, they would invariably return with apologies and a general go-ahead on whatever I intended.

In short, it was a very good life. I would wake up early in the morning, work for an hour or two on my pamphlets (which I had never stopped making), and then head down to the Ministry. Rita would be there. She was always there. Levkin said once that it was likely there was more than one Rita, identical twins or triplets. Whatever the explanation, she was always there, with messages and a bit of repartee. If Levkin had requested me to make a particular inspection, I would go off to that. If not, I would sit around the office for a while, thinking up one or another scheme for the day. For instance, I once decided that all the dog parks in the city should be tested. So, I borrowed a friend's Airedale and went about from dog park to dog park seeing how he liked them. His name was Osip, and he was a rascally dog who was most certainly an expert on how much pleasure could be afforded any particular dog by any particular dog park. Once we had gone from park to park, and I had gotten a general sense of Osip's feelings on the matter, I wrote up a deafening memorandum on the subject, complete with schematics, possible improvements, dog baths, dog bridges, etc. I forwarded this to the Parks Department under the seal of the Seventh Ministry. Within three months, the dog parks had been altered.

For so long I had gone about giving my opinion freely, never supposing that it would be taken. This is a great freedom, and makes it much easier to say whatever comes to one's mind. However, once one's opinion begins to be heeded, well, then one must take a bit of care.

Nevertheless, my career continued. Every Wednesday, before going to the big public library to annotate the permanent copies of the encyclopedia with my own insightful commentary in neat red pen, I would stop down on Bayard Street to visit a Shanghai joint of the old-style called New Green Bo. I was in the middle of eating a plateful of the best vegetable steamed dumplings in the whole city when one of the chefs, a Chinese woman, turned to me. Her face was stern, and I immediately knew she was going to tell me something of great weight.

—Have you heard of the *curling touch*?

—No, I replied.

—Well, she said, when I was a child, we would go often through the countryside to visit my grandmother, who lived near a shrine. She was very old, and lived alone in a country of great rain. In her district, for whatever reason, the waters were always rising. Rain was always on the horizon or coming hard upon one. Lightning figured as certainly as the sun in one's estimation of the sky. It was on one such rainy day that we climbed the gray-green slope leading up to the shrine. Mist clung to the edges of everything, even to our clothing. We trailed little flags of mist as we ran back and forth along the slope. My mother called to us, and her voice was like the hailing of an unknown ship. We called back as though returning from impossible destinations. And up ahead, the light of my grandmother's house. For a moment we were far from it; the slope seemed to go on forever up and up. Then a bank of mist passed before us and passed away again, and there the house was, before us. My grandmother stood at the open door, beckoning. I ran to her, and she lifted me into her arms and said, Today my dear, I am going to tell you about the *curling touch.*

295 We gathered inside and were given something hot to drink and a sort of sweet grain cake to eat, and the fire was stoked, and the door shut. Outside the rain had begun in earnest. In my mother's eyes shone the old happiness that had always been hers when my grandmother was near. Then my grandmother began to speak.

—There was a man, a handsome man. He was not much to look at, no, he was not handsome in that way. No, he was handsome in that he was the beloved of the world. Everything he did went well; everything he touched turned to gold. He was a gambler, but what he did was never gambling, for it seemed impossible that he should ever lose. If he touched a deck of cards, then they were blessed for him. If he lifted knucklebones, then they would only ever fall in patterns betokening victory. His name was Loren Darius.

Now Loren Darius grew to manhood in the bosom of his luck. He lived in a narrow country, and within its confines he grew strong and proud, such that when he departed into the larger world, that place too became fond of him in that peculiar way that seemed to others to be Darius's birthright. Not that his life was unchecked by disaster. His parents had passed away at an early age, leaving him, a boy of five, in the stewardship of his elder sister, who herself passed away before the year was out. Yet even at that age, Loren Darius could not be refused, and when he went to a stream with a fishing pole, or with his bare hands, that stream would give up fish to him, and when he bent over twigs, even in the midst of a storm, fire would rise up to warm him. And so, despite the misfortune of those around him, Loren Darius grew to manhood.

This was an earlier age of the world. You mustn't suppose that things were then as they are now. A city would be such and such a distance by horse, measured by how many nights one would be upon the road. There was less light in general.

Loren Darius traveled widely as a young man, along every frontier he could find. He did not know at the time what he was looking for, but he was troubled by strange dreams. He would fall asleep in a roadside inn or on a village green, or at the margin of a field, and he would dream himself into a hallway. Many doors then, along the hallway. Many doors, and great they were in size and finery. Each night he went farther down the hall, each night opening still another door.

What was behind these doors? None can

say, for Loren refused to speak of it. Yet certainly as time passed he drew closer to what he sought.

Her name was Ilsa Marionette. She was the daughter of Cors Marionette, the famous hunter, he who drove the Corban Bull from Limeu all down to Viruket. You have seen monuments to his bravery. Anyway, it was not long before Ilsa was convinced that her life was with Loren, and not long before Cors was convinced of Loren's grace in the powers of life. For Cors was often heard to say, Strength is nothing, ferocity is a plaything; when life is waged as a war, grace is the only virtue, grace shown through nimbleness. And Loren was certainly nimble. This no one could dispute.

The pair went then back to the small land where Loren was born; they took up a household and her name became Ilsa Darius. It should be remembered too that Ilsa was the fairest woman that had yet walked beneath the sun. Where she went, events of any kind would stop, as men and women alike marveled at her and at her passing by.

And yet despite her beauty and his luck, they did not have between them a profession, for he had been a wanderer, traveling back and forth through the land, and she had been a virtuous daughter, kept indoors away from the mad horde. Some money they had had from her father, but it was not much, and it lasted them only a short while. So, Loren took to traveling to nearby cities, where his luck in gambling might provide them with the money to live.

This strategy proved sound, and for several years the couple lived in great wealth and affluence. Loren would go away to a city, win enormous sums, bring them back to his bride, and live alone with her in the hills some months before leaving again to procure more. And all the time that they were apart they thought only of each other, and it was a terror in the hearts of both that the other should ever come to harm.

One day it came to pass that Loren was returning from a city, his horse and mule heavily laden with his winnings. The day was hot, and the road was a yellow line through the dust. The sun obscured vision and glanced off all it encountered, searing the very ground.

Through it Loren stumbled, leading his horse and mule. Some hours he had been upon the road, and what water he had had been given his mule and horse, for they were bearing a far heavier load then he. Yet he was sore, thirsty, and tired of the sun. Perhaps its weight was even telling upon his mind, for when he saw up ahead a broad tree and shade beneath, he dropped his horse's reins and ran ahead to the shelter of the tree.

As he drew closer Loren saw that a man was there. He looked like some kind of merchant. He was dressed in green, in heavy cloth, even at this hour and heat. The man's horse was behind the tree, grazing in a patch of grass. The man sat, drinking water from a large skin.

Loren approached. Behind him his horse

and mule caught up and passed around the tree to take up with the other horse, and with the green grass there afforded.

—Good day, said Loren.

310 —Sir, said the man, with a slight tinge of a smile. It is a hot day.

—It is that, said Loren, his words spilling out in haste. Could I have some of that water? I gave the last of what I had to my horse and mule, and I have no more. Certainly I can pay you. Gold even.

The man's smile broadened. His features were odd, grand and haughty even as they were drawn and pursed.

—I have no need for gold.

The man had knucklebones in one hand. He was casting them out upon a flat stone, then scooping them up and casting them again.

315 —A wager, then? asked Loren. I would wager anything against you for that skin of water. My horse? My mule?

—I have a horse, said the man. And mules in a stable.

The man unstoppered the wineskin and took another draught of water. This was almost too much for Loren, whose face betrayed his desperation.

—Have you nothing else to wager? asked the man.

And then Loren thought of the one thing that was of worth in his life, the one thing that nothing matched.

—Have you not a wife? asked the merchant.

—I have a wife, said Loren.

Now, never before had he ever considered wagering Ilsa. She was more important to him even than the good fortune that had hitherto sheltered him. But it was true that he had never lost a wager in his life.

—Then let us say, said the merchant, this skin of water set against your wife. Ilsa, her name is, no?

Loren drew back. How did the man know her name?

—She is a noted beauty in these parts, the merchant said, answering Loren's unspoken question.

Loren drew in a deep breath. He could win this with a single throw, get the water, take the horse and mule, and be home by nightfall. It would be over in a moment. He would be hazarding her only for a moment.

The man lifted the skin to his lips again. Soon the water would be gone.

Loren reached out his hand.

—Let's have it. Come now.

The merchant took from beneath his green coat a tattered leather cup. Into it he dropped the bones and handed them to Loren. Loren felt in himself a great unease. He looked into the merchant's face and was terrified by what he saw there. He knew then that he should stop. He felt a horror in himself and in the world.

He threw the bones down onto the flat rock.

They skipped out and landed in that series known as "bird's teeth." It was the second-best throw. Never before had Loren failed to get the best throw. But "bird's teeth" was a good throw.

The merchant's hands moved almost faster than Loren could see, scooping up the bones, dropping them into the cup, and passing them over the rock once, twice, three times. On the third pass he let them slide out and drop, one two three four five. They dropped slowly, perfectly into the "widow's net," the very best throw. Loren had lost.

With a cry he threw up his hands.

—This is foolishness, he said. I am leaving.

The merchant stood up to his full height, and he was a large man indeed. The dice cup fell from his hand.

—Loren Darius, I know you. I have known you long, and long you have been kept from my hand. But now my weight is upon you and I will never relent. Ilsa Darius is mine. I may not come for her today; I may not come tomorrow. I may not come for years. But when I do there will be nothing you can do. For on this day you have lost her to me. On this day you have given your wife for a skin of water.

The man turned and called out in a strange voice. His horse trotted up beside him. The man walked away down the road as Loren watched, and after he was gone a dozen paces, a fold of heat and light arose and the man was lost to sight.

At this, Loren stirred. He leaped onto his horse's back and, forgetting the mule, rode at breakneck speed the remaining miles home.

As he came up the path to his house, his horse foaming and lathering, he saw upon the porch, Ilsa. She was singing and singing the song he had heard every night in his dreams as he woke again and again into that grave hallway.

He leaped from off his horse and ran up the steps.

—Ilsa, he cried. Ilsa, are you well? Have there been any visitors?

And Ilsa looked at him strangely even as he caught her up in his arms.

—No, my love. No visitors. Only your absence, and your return.

Loren breathed a sigh of relief. It must have been a dream, he thought, a dream prompted by the heat. Yet when he looked down at his wrist he saw a mark, a mark as of a burn where the man had touched him when taking the leather cup in his turn. *The curling touch.* Loren had heard of it. He had not dreamed the wager. Yet who was this man? If he came here, Loren would slay him. That was all. He would slay the man.

And so their life continued. Things continued as they had, and Loren and Ilsa were glad in their days. Yet sometimes Loren would think that he heard things or saw things. He would be returning from a trip to gather wood and he would think he saw a man leaving the house. Or he would see from afar in the window of the bedroom a man's shape. Always he would run to the house and come shouting in, to find poor Ilsa all alone, seemingly confused at what had aroused her husband to such madness.

She bore such things well, yet as time went on, the occurrences began to come with greater and greater frequency. Loren would search the house from top to bottom. But never would he find anyone there, or anything not as it should have been. As had happened repeatedly in the past, the couple began to run out of money. But now, instead of going off to the city as he had before, Loren refused to leave the house. He was sure that as soon as he left, the man would come. Yet their money dwindled, and their food, and soon there was nothing for it but that he go.

So Loren left one day, and went along the road to the nearest city. There he stayed six days gambling, and raised such a fortune as he had never seen. He took two mules and his good horse and set out home. Yet with each mile that passed, his anxiety increased, and it was all he could do not to cast aside the slower mules and gallop home.

As he came up the path to his house he saw tracks left by a horse not his own. When he reached the house, he found Ilsa sitting, wearing clothes he had not seen before. And so his greeting to her was not, as it had been, My love, how I have missed you, or Darling, how are you, but:

—Who gave you that dress? And what horse left tracks upon the path? You have had visitors; I know it.

Ilsa told him that it was a woman who lived nearby, who had come several times to see her, for it grows lonely here when no one is around.

To which Loren said, you have never grown lonely before.

And she replied, always before you have been here with me, even when you were not.

Then they both saw that something deep and terrible had happened. But they did not know how to fix it, or even how to name it.

The mark on Loren's wrist remained. The money he had made was enough to continue their life for a very long time without his going away. Yet still, he would go down into the meadow past the house, where a narrow path wound through trees to a brook, and the Cassila, with its flowering branches raves in good pleasure all through the spring, and even there, there with the bouquet of scent, the dazing pleasuring sunlight, the rushing swiftness of the brook, and the standing comfort of the grasses, he felt at his core the beginnings of a slight terror. It was then he would turn to the house and would see, or hear from afar, as though he were near, the sound of Ilsa's lovemaking as she lay with another man, the sound of her calling out, the rustling of sheets, the noise of skin and skin.

He would rush, blue veined in anger, up the stairs, to find her at needlework by a window, or weaving in the parlor. Yet there would be to her then some slight disarray, a looseness to her hair, a flush to her lips, a half-buttoned dress or an uncaught breath, that to him would cement all his fears.

In his dreams, both waking and sleeping, he was forced to watch as different men, not just the merchant, but others, came to his wife, and she to them. Finally Loren's angers grew too great, and Ilsa fled the house in the company of a friend she knew only slightly, a girl she had encountered once, the supposed daughter of woman she knew. They fled to a nearby village, pursued by Loren, and took shelter in the uppermost room of an inn.

Loren rode that day desperately after her. He remembered how it had been in what seemed now like their youth. He thought of her gentleness, her tenderness with him always, and how quick she had been in thought, yet always thinking of him. And as he rode, his anger softened, and he felt in his heart that he had wronged her. Yet then by chance his eye passed over the reins and over his wrist and he beheld there the raging mark, the burn of which he felt still, and with it his anger grew.

He made his way into the town and cast his luck in the air. It sent him to the inn. He tied his horse to a pole, threw open the door, and entered. A great many people were in the common room. A young man in a blue-gray suit. A woman with a fan. An old man whose age lay all about his feet, and a tall man tall with a broad, kind face, a black beard, black eyes and hair, a dog on hind legs holding a violin. The black-bearded man took Loren by the shoulder. He said,

—You think that by going upstairs, the 360
world will continue. But there is more to it than that. He wants to go upstairs, said the man, pointing to the young fellow in the blue-gray suit, but he isn't going. He's staying right here. You sit here a moment.

Loren sat. His mind was in a seething fury.

The young man in the blue-gray suit came over and patted him on the shoulder.

—My friend, he said, this is for you.

He pressed an orange into Loren's hand. But it was not just any orange. It was the orange that Loren had been about to eat when news had come to him of his parents' death. How had the orange been preserved so long? How could it still be fresh? Yet it was. Loren peeled the orange, and it was as perfect a fruit as he had ever seen. He took a portion and put it in his mouth, and the taste filled him. It was full of freshness and new promise, the lifting of obligation. He gave pieces of the orange to everyone in the room, and they all ate, smiling.

The young man knelt by Loren and whis- 365
pered in his ear:

—Though we pass away now, the world will return to you again; fear not.

For at that moment the black-bearded blacksmith began to speak, and all that he said became more and more certain until only his subject remained.

—I heard tell once, he was saying, of a guess artist. He lived in a grand and impossible city, a place not out of a true future, but an imagined future. There were great wings that propelled men in gatherings through the sky, and tall, tall houses, called skyscrapers. In the water too there were massive ships that circumnavigated the world, bearing goods in trade. So many people lived in the city that they were forced to live atop one another. Houses atop houses atop houses. When the people went out into the street, there was one unending crowd through which they went and in which they lived.

There were many nations in the world, and all were linked, and the populace of this one city was composed of many of the peoples of the earth. Where this city met the ocean, on its southeast border, there was a great wooden plank-land, planks stretching out along the coast. They called it a boardwalk. And upon the boardwalk, the man of whom I speak, the guess artist, had a stand. Late in the day, when the heat had faded somewhat into the planks of the boardwalk and down into the sand that lay all around, he would take up his position in a tent behind a small counter adjoining the boardwalk, there to wait for customers.

The place was lit by electric light, something like the lightning that comes now from the sky, but harnessed, and set into veins called power lines. This energy was free to be used by anyone, and then night was not the serious affair that it is now. Lights lit the streets, lit the insides of buildings, and light lit the boardwalk, clear from one end of Coney Island to the other.

On this particular day the guess artist was

sitting, looking out across the water, when a young Japanese couple approached. Across the way, a young man in a blue-gray suit had been waiting some time. The guess artist knew that the young man wanted to come to speak with the guess artist, but something was keeping him away.

The young Japanese couple looked at the guess artist's brochure. It was a flat card that said,

—In three guesses I will guess what you are thinking.

—How much does it cost? asked Takashi Kawagata.

—You will give me what you think I 375
deserve, said the guess artist.

—That sounds fair, said June Kawagata. What am I thinking?

—You are both thinking the same thing, said the guess artist. You are wondering whether the sun will ever go down, since you have been traveling now for six years on airplanes, staying ahead of the sun, and you have finally decided today to let yourselves see a sunset.

—That's not true, said June. I design robots for use in private industry. We have an apartment on the West Side.

—Okay, said the guess artist. Three chances, right?

—Okay, said June. Shoot. 380

—You're thinking about the cat you had when you were a child. There was one spot on its fur, to the left of its tail, which would never sit smoothly. The fur always stuck up. Somehow you thought that because the fur was always sticking up there, the world could never reward anyone with exactly what they wanted. This belief was for a long time unconscious in your head, but earlier today you realized why you believe what you believe. Furthermore, now you feel that it is certainly true. The cat died when you were nine. It is buried by the gate of your parents' house in Tensshu.

—What is the cat's name? asked June.

—You are being very careful not to think of the cat's name, said the guess artist.

Then his expression changed. He looked at Takashi.

—The cat's name was Octopus.

June gave Takashi a withering look.

—Don't you have any self-control? she asked.

Takashi shrugged.

June looked at the guess artist.

—You're pretty good, she said. What do you think?

—About what? he asked.

—About the patch of fur, she said.

—I think you're right about the patch of fur. I could have told you more if you had brought Octopus here.

—But I was only a kid then. I didn't know about you.

—I know, said the guess artist.

Takashi took a chocolate-chip cookie wrapped very carefully in waxed paper out of his bag. It was obviously from an extremely expensive cookie boutique uptown. He gave it to the guess artist.

—Thank you, said the guess artist.

—See you around, said June and Takashi.

The guess artist watched them walk off down the boardwalk. What a nice couple, he thought to himself.

At that moment, the young man in the gray- 400
blue suit approached the guess artist's booth. He was a serious young man with a way of moving that said, I am trying to be extraordinarily quiet right now even though it makes no difference.

—Hello, said the guess artist.

—Hello, said the young man.

—When you were standing over by the railing you were thinking about the time you parachuted from a small prop plane. It was your first time, and so you had to have someone jump with you, attached to your back. Nonetheless, the experience was wonderful. The day was slightly cloudy, and so you fell through hundreds of wisps of cloud, to emerge into an open sky over the Hudson Valley.

—Not really, said the young man.

The guess artist raised an eyebrow. 405

—Earlier today, I thought about that, said the young man. Just now I thought about how I had been thinking about that, to be precise. And anyway, the thing isn't what I was thinking about when I was standing over there. It's what I'm thinking about right now.

—True, said the guess artist. Give me a minute.

He looked at the young man again. Perhaps he resembled an animal that had been turned into a human being by some accident, and now was trying to make the best of the situation. Yes, said the guess artist to himself, that's the way it is.

—Well . . . said the young man.

410 —You're looking for a girl, said the guess artist. You had hoped she would be on the boardwalk, but she's not. She's upstairs somewhere, you think, though you don't know where.

—Well, said the young man again, I think—

—But, continued the guess artist, you're worried that you won't be able to find her alone, and in truth, you will not be able to find her alone. She is too hard to find. You will need help. Somehow you knew that I was the only one who could help you. That's why you've come here every day for the last week and stood over there watching me. Also, just now you noticed my chocolate-chip cookie and you want a bite. Ask me for a piece.

—Can I have a piece of your chocolate-chip cookie? asked the young man.

—Yes, said the guess artist. And, I will help you find this girl.

415 He broke the cookie into two halves. When he did this, the cookie broke beautifully. The substance it was made of was quite obviously the most extraordinary substance that one could make a chocolate-chip cookie from and still call it a chocolate-chip cookie. The two ate the cookie in silence. When they were done, the young man said,

—That's the best chocolate-chip cookie I have ever eaten, or seen.

—Let's go, said the guess artist. There isn't much time. Do you have anything to show me, any clues to where she might be?

The young man slid an envelope out of his sleeve. He did it so quickly and well that the guess artist smiled at the artfulness of the gesture. There was a letter in the envelope. It said:

Hey, you,

I'm in a hurry, so I can't write much. Meet me at Pier 12 at four a.m. two nights from now. Is there such a thing as useless obfuscation? I don't think so.

Resolutely yours,

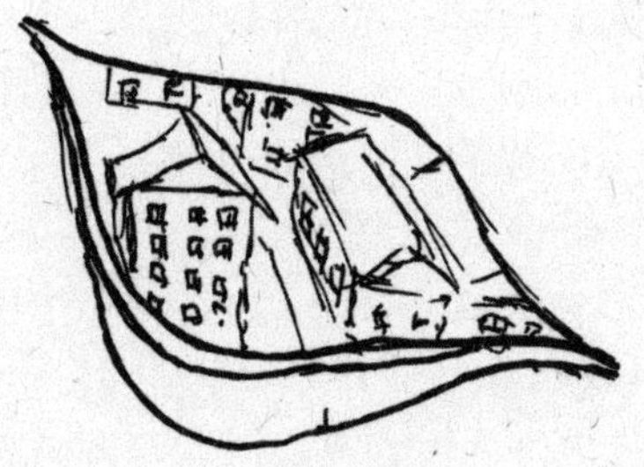

---

420 —Hmmm, said the guess artist. What happened when you went to the pier?

—It was very strange, said the young man.

At this the guess artist straightened up in his chair. The young man did not seem like the sort of person who used the word *strange* lightly.

—When I got there, there was some kind of selection process going on. There were many girls, all dressed alike in white linen sundresses. Also, they all looked vaguely like Her. But they weren't Her. None of them was Her. Some of them even, while they were waiting for their turn to talk to the judges, made little gestures reminiscent of Her. But they were clearly not Her. I waited until they all spoke to the judges. Then I spoke to the judges. Then everyone left. Then I left.

—What did the judges say?

425 —They said that I seemed very confused and that I should have that looked at. Also they said they were going to have a drink and that if I wanted I could come along.

—What did they look like?

—The judges?

—Yes, said the guess artist.

—More of the same, said the young man. They looked perhaps even more like Her than the contestants.

430 —Hmmm, said the guess artist. And they didn't say why they were there?

—There was a handbill, said the young man. He took it out of his other sleeve and gave it to the guess artist. The handbill was blank.

—Very interesting, said the guess artist.

He took a little bottle of rubbing alcohol from a cabinet that was hidden behind the counter and poured a little over the handbill. Letters emerged. The handbill now said:

Pier 12, four a.m. Look-alike contest.

—Did you go back the next night? asked 435
the guess artist.

—Yes, there was a different contest. Everyone then also looked vaguely similar, but not to anyone I knew.

—Well, there's only one thing for it, said the guess artist. Let's go to the dead-letter office. There may be more correspondence for you there.

The guess artist came around the counter, turned, pulled the curtain to, and the new comrades headed off down the boardwalk in the direction of Manhattan. It was a fine night, and the people passing them all seemed happy in general about some unverified thing. The municipal inspector thought to himself that it was good in many ways that he did not know what this thing was, for perhaps in himself he carried the disproof of it, and that perhaps his knowing the falseness of their happiness would make it no longer real, whereas now it was real, real for them, and for him, protected by a veil of not-knowing. Meanwhile beside him the guess artist knew very well what it was about which the people were happy, but he did not let himself think about it. In his head were many obscure structures for protecting himself from the thoughts of others.

They reached the subway platform and boarded the train, when it came, in silence. The municipal inspector sat beside the guess artist, and they looked out the window over Brighton Beach as the train sped west.

—What should I call you? asked the guess artist.

—S. is fine, said the young man in the gray-blue suit.

—S. it is, then, said the guess artist. Why is it that this girl needs to be found in the first place?

—Because, said S., she has lost her memory.

—Ah! said the guess artist decisively. Ah ha!

Across the way, a large building slid by. There was an open window on the third floor. A girl was leaning out of it and waving at the train. It was almost certainly the girl whom S. was looking for. But S. was looking elsewhere. Only the guess artist saw her.

—What? asked S.

—Well, if she has lost her memory, then I think I know how she can be found.

—Do tell, said S.

—By reconstructing her entire past. But

first, let's look at the dead-letter office. There may be something there.

The train continued on its rambling way 450
through Brooklyn and into Manhattan. The pair alighted at Thirty-fourth Street and made their way down to the enormous post office that sits like a behemoth in that section of the city.

Crossing Eighth Avenue, the guess artist asked the municipal inspector how they would manage to enter the post office at this late hour. To which the municipal inspector laughed and explained that he was a municipal inspector. To which the guess artist explained that he knew that already, but nonetheless, did there not exist the chance that his badge would not be taken seriously? To which the municipal inspector said that it was better not to think of that, at least for the moment.

By that time they were up the steps and knocking on the front door. A guard came up with a flashlight.

—Who are you? he asked. What do you want?

S. held up his badge. The guard examined it, and unlocked the door. Opening it, he said,

455 —All right, well, come on in.

S. did a slight bow in the guard's direction, then continued past him into the post office.

—Do you know where we're going? he asked the guess artist quietly.

—Not really, said the guess artist. Give me a moment.

He looked in the direction of the security guard, who was examining the lock mechanism on the door. He closed his eyes for a second, then opened them.

460 —This way, he said.

—Did you just . . . ? asked S.

—Better not to think about it, said the guess artist.

They continued down a short stairwell to a lower level, then along a ramp, through a double door, into a right-angling hallway, through a sort of auditorium, and then up to a large locked door. Beside it was a bell.

The guess artist stopped in front of the bell.

465 —I think it's important that you ring the bell. We don't want to mess this up.

—You're right, said S. Do you remember what Ref the Sly said to his mother when he returned from killing Thorbjorn?

—It was a riddle, but I don't remember

what, said the guess artist, unhappy that he had been caught forgetful of his sagas.

—He says that he probed the path to his heart. Also he says that he was offered a knife and a whetstone. I think Thorbjorn had it coming, don't you?

—Probably, said the guess artist.

S. pulled very hard on the bell cord. The resulting sound was quite loud, but neither of them stirred an inch. The municipal inspector was thinking about the girl and how she had lost her memory because of being hit by a taxi. The guess artist was thinking that the municipal inspector was thinking of the Thomas Gray poem that goes

Perhaps in this neglected spot is laid
Some heart once pregnant with celestial fire;
Hands, that the rod of empire might have sway'd,
Or wak'd to ecstasy the living lyre.

The guess artist was touched very much by this. He thought it wonderful that the municipal inspector should admire also a verse of which he was so fond.

But, of course, he was wrong. The municipal inspector was thinking about how it was strange that Mora had managed to land entirely upon her head, and did things like that happen to her often? Perhaps they did, and if so, was she a good person to know? Perhaps not.

A little metal window slid open, and someone's eye was looking at them.

—What do you want?

—Is this the dead-letter office? asked S.

—Are you asking me? asked the dead-letter clerk.

—I suppose, said S.

—Then come back tomorrow. At this hour, we only deal with implacable demands, particularly those enforced with fists and knives.

He shut the metal window, and his footsteps were audible as he walked away from the door.

S. rang the bell again. After a moment, the footsteps could be heard again. Again the window slid open.

—What do you want?

The man's voice was a little whiny.

—Let us in, said S. I'm an Inspector.

He showed his badge again.

The metal window slid shut, and they could hear locks being unbound. Slowly the door swung open.

—Well, come on in. You're the first visitors in a long while, said the dead-letter clerk.

He was a tiny man, with a long face, long fingers, and a keen gaze like a lamp.

—We're looking for— began the guess artist.

—Don't tell me, said the clerk. You'll see why.

He led them down a low hallway, so low

that S. and the guess artist were forced to duck their heads as they walked. At the end there was a step down and a turn. As they came around the turn, they beheld an enormous room the size of a gymnasium. The entire room was piled high with letters of every kind. One huge pile of letters, perhaps two stories tall. Up above, on the ceiling, there was some kind of aperture that opened and closed. Through it, the guess artist surmised, the letters were dropped by some kind of machine.

On the far side there was a bed, a table, some chairs, a little bookshelf, a single burner, and a sink strapped to the wall.

—Do you live here? asked S.

—We do, said the clerk. My wife and I.

A woman came out from behind the pile of letters. She looked identical to the dead-letter clerk except that she had long hair.

—Hello, she said.

Her voice was very pleasant. As soon as she said hello, both the guess artist and S. wanted very much for her to say something else.

—How are you? they asked.

—All right, she said. We have the devil at our necks down here. If we don't get something done with these letters, our home will be crushed.

And indeed it was true. The letters were already encroaching on the area where their little home was situated.

—Whose idea was it to put your things there? asked S.

505 —The director's, said the clerk. It's to boost productivity.

—But what are you supposed to do with the letters? asked the guess artist.

—We have to get rid of them somehow, said the clerk's wife. I often put them into other envelopes.

She took some out of her pocket.

—And then I mail them to other places.

510 —What do you do with them? the guess artist asked the clerk.

—I like to cut them up into bits and put them in the tube.

In one wall there was a large tube mouth. The clerk held up a set of cunningly fashioned shears. They looked like they would cut through almost anything.

—Those look like they could cut through almost anything, said the municipal inspector.

The clerk picked up a metal pipe that happened to be lying on the floor. He nipped at it with the shears and cut it in half.

515 —Pretty neat, said S.

—Thanks, said the clerk, blushing.

The clerk's wife came over and patted him on the shoulder.

—He's very proud of his shears. He just got them a week ago.

—A week ago? asked the guess artist.

520 —Yes, just a week ago, she said. It was his birthday.

At this the dead-letter clerk blushed even more.

—Well, happy birthday, said S.

—Thank you, said the clerk.

He looked down at his feet for a while and then managed to regain his composure.

—Was there anything you wanted down here? he said.

—We're looking for any letters having to do with a girl, said S. carefully.

—Hmmm, said the clerk's wife.

It was a really wonderful hmmm, and the other three smiled gently at the sound of it.

—Do you know her name? she continued.

—No, said S. She lost her memory and I'm in charge of finding it.

—A special case, then, said the clerk. I wonder if . . .

—Good idea! said the guess artist.

—What? said the dead-letter clerk.

—He's a guess artist, said S. Sometimes he can guess what you're thinking.

—Really? asked the clerk's wife. Would you try to guess what I'm thinking? she asked softly.

—Sure I would, said the guess artist.

He looked at her for a while.

—You want to take a trip to the country, but you're afraid that if you say so your husband might be sad because he loves it so in the dead-letter office, and doesn't really want to go anywhere else, and besides, you know that if you left, the work would pile up and you might come back and have nowhere to sleep and what would you do then?

—How did you know? she said, aghast.

—You want to leave? said the clerk to his wife. His eyes got very large and began to fill up with tears.

—Just for a few days, she said. Just for a weekend. You know, a weekend in the country!

Her face was radiant. She really did look not at all like him sometimes, and just like him other times.

—But, he said, the letters . . .

—I know, she said. Don't worry. We're not going anywhere.

There was not a trace of resentment in her voice.

—Now, she said, turning back, what are we going to do about your girl's lost memory?

—I had an idea, said the clerk, but I seem to have forgotten it.

—It was, said the guess artist, that you were going to use the dog to sniff the letter out.

—Dog? asked S.

—Whirligig! called out the clerk.

From the top of the pile of mail came bounding a miniature German shepherd. He was perfect in every way, but very tiny. He ran up to the clerk, who knelt down to receive him. The two exchanged greetings.

—Do you have anything that belonged to the girl? asked the clerk's wife. A sock? A scarf?

—I have her shoe, said S.

Out of a secret pocket he produced one of the two espadrilles that the girl was wearing during the accident.

—What a nice shoe, said the clerk's wife.

—You were carrying that all along? asked the guess artist.

—No, said S. It just occurred to me now.

The clerk held the espadrille for the dog to smell. He sniffed at it with his nose, then ran away into the pile of letters. Sometimes he climbed and sometimes he swam through them. Soon he had disappeared from sight.

—If anyone can find it, said the clerk, Whirligig can. He's quite a pup.

—Where did you get him? asked S.

—He was in a package that came here, said the guess artist. She heard barking coming out of a box; she opened it up, and there he was.

—Actually, said the clerk's wife, he was a gift from my sister, who lives in Idaho.

—But how did he arrive? asked the guess artist. Truthfully, now.

—In a box, said the clerk's wife. Wrapped up in a sweater.

—That's no way to send a dog, said S.

—But in this case, said the clerk, it worked just fine.

—Nobody's disputing that, said S.

—The other day, said the guess artist, I was down by the harbor and I saw the most horrible sight.

Everyone looked at him.

570 —A seagull was flying about, as seagulls often do. However, this one tried to fly beneath a dock, and it fetched up against one of the wooden supports. It must have broken its wing, because it fell there, right in the shallows, and was splashing around but going nowhere. Out from beneath the dock then came a large swan. It came closer and closer to the seagull, came right up over it and began to tear at the seagull with its beak. It started tearing off pieces of the seagull, eating it while it was still alive. I've never seen anything like it.

—That's horrible, said the dead-letter clerk.

—I wish I had never heard that, said the dead-letter clerk's wife.

S. nodded slowly to himself; he knew well the true nature of swans.

Just at that moment, Whirligig reappeared from the pile. He was carrying two letters in his dandy little mouth. He ran up to S. and dropped them at his feet. S. patted him on the head and picked up the letters.

575 The first letter came in a richly embroidered envelope. There were traces of gold in the fibers of the paper, and the address had actually been embroidered on. It said, *Selah Morse, God Knows Where.* He put that envelope on the bottom and picked up the other. It was a simple white envelope, one of the official sort that you buy at the post office, where the letter folds into being the envelope. This one said nothing on the outside. He opened it.

---

14 Beard Street
Brooklyn, NY

Soon.

Or else.

He narrowed his eyes.

—Very strange, he said, and his voice was loud in his ears.

—We had best be going, said the guess artist.

—But the other letter, said the clerk's wife.

—It's from his sister, said the guess artist. She died some time ago. I don't know that he was ever meant to see that letter.

—Then give it back to me, said the clerk's wife. She took a hold of the letter and began to pull it out of S.'s hand.

—No! said S. That's my letter. Let go!

The two were pulling back and forth on the letter. Whirligig began to bark and nip at the ankles of S. and the guess artist. Just at that moment, the aperture in the ceiling opened and letters began to pour in, pouring down over the pile, increasing its size with every second. The noise was tremendous. Also, the clerk began to shout.

The clerk's wife pulled the letter away from S. and ran off. He chased after her, but she was very fast, and also good at running on top of piled letters, which S. was not. She made it away past a sort of small portcullis, which she brought down immediately. S. halted before it.

—I'll be back for that letter, he said.

—Not on your life, she said. My husband's going to cut it up with his shears.

—You wouldn't do that, would you? asked S.

590 But the clerk was running around in circles, shouting and trying to save his home from the incoming flood, with Whirligig at, before, and around his heels. The mail continued to pour out of the ceiling at an increasing rate.

—We've got to go, said the guess artist.

—I guess you're right, said S.

Together they ran, half-bent over so their heads wouldn't knock against the low ceiling, back up one passage, then another, and out of the lower reaches of the post office.

As they reached the main level, they stopped, huffing and puffing, to catch their breath. The security guard came out of an alcove and shone a light on them. Everything was very quiet and still. None of the chaos they had seen below existed here.

595 —Odd down there, isn't it? he asked. I never go down there after dark.

—Who's in charge of this place? asked S.

—There's a big computer somewhere, said the guard, made out of wood. That's what they make computers out of nowadays, the really fast ones, anyway.

—Right, said the guess artist. Well, goodbye.

Out, then, the front doors, and into the night.

—Should we go to the address now? asked S.

—It seemed urgent, said the guess artist. Not much else to be done about it, don't you think? Do you know where to go?

—I do, said S.

The two were quiet a moment. S.'s hands were making a sad expression, one not betrayed by his face or eyes.

—I wonder what that letter said.

—Probably something kind and useless, said the guess artist. You can assume that much.

The guess artist patted the municipal inspector on the shoulder.

They went down through the pavement and through a turnstile. A subway car drew up immediately, as though it had been waiting for them. The guess artist wondered how long it had been waiting there. The municipal inspector thought some more about his sister's letter and how horrible it was that he hadn't gotten to read it.

They sat down. The train began to move.

The municipal inspector took something out of his sleeve. He unfolded it, and as he unfolded it, it became bigger and bigger. The whole thing was covered in child's writing. It was in red crayon, with occasional blue and green. S. looked at it intently. He mumbled to himself and moved his finger over it slowly.

The train passed on at great speed.

—This must be the express, said the guess artist.

S. murmured something noncommittal.

—What is that? asked the guess artist.

—A map, said S.

—Of what? asked the guess artist.

—Can't you guess? asked S., a bit brusquely.

He was still bothered by the loss of his sister's letter. Should he go back and try to claim it later? he wondered to himself. No, no, it was lost forever. He shook his head and returned to the matter at hand.

The guess artist was peering at him.

—No, I can't, he said. Where this map is concerned your mind is . . . blurry. I can't tell a thing.

—Well, it IS an odd business, said S.

He pointed to a spot on the map.

—We're here, he said.

The guess artist nodded.

—Is that me? he asked.

There was a drawing of a man with question marks shooting out of his head. As the guess artist looked closer at the drawing, it seemed to get larger and more detailed. He could almost make out his face.

—Yes, said S., that's you. Do you know how déjà vu occurs?

—No, said the guess artist.

—Well, said S., when you are a child, somewhere between two and four years of age, a night comes that you have a dream. In that dream you dream your entire life, from start to finish, with all its happinesses, its disappointments, its loves, its hates, its pains, its joys. Your entire life. The dream should have to last an equivalent amount of time, but somehow it happens in just one night.

The guess artist said nothing, but only stared at S. with a look of great and involved interest. This pleased S. He continued.

—Most people forget their dream. In fact, 630
everyone forgets most of it. However, I was a precocious child. That morning I was left alone by myself with a large sheet of paper and a bucket of crayons. While my dream was still fresh in my head, I constructed a map of my life, using symbols and writing down what I could. Somehow I realized that to write too much would ruin it, and would make me sad in the end. Therefore, what I wrote down were mostly clues as to how to manage the difficult parts.

He closed the map up and returned it to his sleeve.

—Doesn't that make life rather complicated? asked the guess artist.

—I don't think it can become more complicated than it is. I think it has already inherently reached the ultimate level of complication.

—What does it say about our search? asked the guess artist.

635 —We're coming up to a tricky part. I think we may end up in a bit of trouble for a little while.

—All right, said the guess artist. I don't mind that. I don't have anything else to do. And I can always go back to my booth.

—Yes, said S. You can always go back to your booth.

Just then the train pulled into a station. The municipal inspector and the guess artist got off. They went down to the street level and walked for a while in the direction of Beard Street. The night had been passed in great industry and first false, then true exaggeration of circumstance. Both men felt this, and it was a pleasing feeling. The sun was coming up behind them to the left as they walked, and they could feel it warming their backs. The guess artist thought of his booth, and how the light would be warming the curtain that hung over it, how an old man might be walking along the boardwalk just at this moment, and how he might look at the guess artist's sign and think, I wonder if he can guess my thought. The guess artist tried, just to try.

—He is thinking of his late wife, who used to love to drink tea when the sun was rising. All the rest of the day for her was naught. Just drinking tea at dawn and having a bit of a walk to look for signs that the seasons were changing. And also there was the picture of her when she was a young woman and all the young men were after her for a date. And how she had asked him, *she* had asked *him,* if he wanted to go on the Ferris wheel, and how fine it had been that night, with all the lights of Manhattan far away on the horizon, and the feel of his own body, young in his young man's clothes.

—What are you talking about? asked S.

—Nothing, said the guess artist. Here we are.

Up ahead there was a sign.

BEARD STREET

it said.

—It's that way, said S., pointing to the left.

They walked along for a little ways. It was a Victorian house, quite a large one, standing all by itself on an overgrown block. There was a high stone wall around the premises. Farther down the street, S. could see the warehouses where ships would leave their goods, and the wharves. He could see in the distance Governors Island and the Statue of Liberty. Lower Manhattan sat quietly too, behind a veil of Brooklyn buildings. He thought then of the Seventh Ministry, of Rita sitting behind her desk, delicately writing out messages to bring up to him upon his return. He thought too of Mars Levkin, who might be wondering at that very moment just what the young inspector was up to.

Well, Levkin, thought S., I think you would approve.

—In we go, said S.

Up to the gate he proceeded. A metal plate was stamped and set upon the gate: 14 BEARD STREET, it said. He unbolted the gate, and passed through. The guess artist followed after. Up the stone stair they went to the door. S. knocked upon the door. There was no answer. However, there was certainly the hush of something about to happen, and the hush of a large number of people suddenly deciding en masse to keep quiet.

—What on earth? asked the guess artist.

650 S. closed his eyes a moment, took a deep breath, and stepped through the door. The interior of the house was somewhat dark. All the windows had been covered over, and lamps gave what little light there was.

—Hello! he said. Is there anyone here?

The guess artist came to his side.

—Many people are thinking, he said. But they are being very quiet, even about that.

A loud noise of bolting came behind them. S. spun around. The door had been shut. A large man stood in front of it, barring their way.

655 —So you thought you'd come to Fourteen Beard Street? he said in a booming voice. Many people come, but no one has ever left. It is a sort of trap. We let people in. Anyone can come in. The door is often open. But once you are in, you are in. You may live here, happily. People have lived happy lives within the confines of this house. We have a small population here. Imminently, you will be introduced around. I myself will perform this service for you.

He was wearing a scarlet dressing gown, and his fists were the sort of fists an oak tree might have if it balled up its roots and decided to hit you.

—I'm surprised, said the guess artist.

—Where is the girl? asked S.

—All your questions will be answered, or unanswered in time. For now, come and sit in the study. We shall have a cigar and talk of old times. If I am not mistaken, we know each other.

—I don't remember that, said S., but let's get along. The sooner we learn the facts of the matter, the better.

—Facts of the matter! snorted the man. You can't leave; that's the only fact. Haven't you read Dumas? Haven't you heard of *the mousetrap*? Everyone who enters the building is held there indefinitely. This is the only real mousetrap there's ever been.

—Clearly insane, whispered the guess artist in S.'s ear.

—What is he thinking? asked S. quietly.

—He's thinking about flying a plane over a broad and tumultuous sea.

—Really? asked S.

—And the strangest thing is, the plane is shaped just like this house.

They came to the study. The man ushered them in. They sat in comfortable chairs. On the wall were many fine paintings, mostly impressionist.

—You like the French? asked S.

—I like vague things, said the man. The vaguer the better.

He turned to the door.

—You can come in now! he bellowed. It's safe!

Dozens of people, it seemed then, came running into the room, and as they did, the room grew larger to fit them. Or had the room been that large from the beginning? That was the only explanation. The people were all dressed as children, in odd nineteenth-century clothing. They had shrill voices, and made braying noises with their throats as they ran.

S. and the guess artist looked at each other in horror and drew back in their chairs.

—Just my little joke, said the man.

He clapped his hands and all the children went away. The room was empty again and small.

—Caroline, he called. We have guests.

A finely dressed woman in her forties entered the room.

—Patrick, she said, you should have told me we were having guests.

She gave him a sharp look.

The guess artist leaned over and whispered in S.'s ear.

—The plane just landed.

—Hello, said Caroline. I'm the mistress of the house. Can I get you something, a cold drink, perhaps?

—Yes, said S., I would like a cup of water, if it's not too much trouble.

—For me too, said the guess artist.

—All right, said Caroline in an angry voice.

If you want some goddamned water, you had best go and get it for yourselves. What do you think I am? Your maid?

Patrick looked very angry as well.

—Who do you think you are, he asked, coming into my house and ordering my wife around? Did I even invite you here? I think not.

S. held up the letter from the dead-letter office. Immediately, Patrick and Caroline grew quiet.

—Where did you get that? they asked.

—It doesn't matter, said the guess artist. We have it, and we're here. Where is the girl?

Caroline and Patrick left the room.

—I'm afraid we may be stuck here a very long time, said S. My map indicated something unfortunate was going to happen.

—You may be right, said the guess artist.

Patrick and Caroline came back in. Both of them had changed their clothing. To what purpose, S. could not say.

—I suppose we got off on the wrong foot, said Caroline. Now, do either of you want anything to drink? Something cold, perhaps?

—Nothing for me, said S.

—Nothing for me either, said the guess artist.

—Good, good, she said. Well, let's get down to business. I want you to have a nice stay here.

She smiled and crossed her legs. It occurred to S. that her legs were on backwards. Or for a moment they had been, but now they were on right again. He looked up at the man, who was carving something out of a piece of wood. He was completely intent on this, and did not seem to notice that S. was looking at him. What was he carving? thought S. It looked like a wolf, but it had a fish body.

The man looked up.

—It's a sea-wolf, he said. They are very hungry all the time.

—I would expect that, said S.

—Well, we'll leave you for a while, said Caroline. The other guests come and go—well, not from the house, I mean, but from the various rooms, so you should be meeting them shortly, or eventually, if you get my meaning. Anyway, good-bye. Ring that bell if you want one of the servants to bring anything.

On the wall beside a bust of Verlaine, there was a bell cord.

—I shall, said S.

Caroline and Patrick left the room. As they left, Patrick asked Caroline what color the sea-wolf should be, and Caroline told Patrick that sea-wolves are black with yellow blood, and that they are cowards at heart. At this Patrick became very quiet, even while he was walking. Now, it is not an easy task to become *that* quiet while walking, but he managed it.

Almost as soon as the couple had left, the guess artist and the municipal inspector became conscious of someone else in the room. A man was sitting in the corner by a lamp, reading a book. He wore a long beard in white, and was dressed as one imagined an old gentleman might have dressed in the year 1927 in the city of Warsaw. The old man noticed their attention, and looked up.

—Good afternoon, he said.

—Is it afternoon? asked the guess artist.

—Only just, he said. Allow me to introduce myself. My name is Piers Golp.

—I'm Selah Morse, said S. And this fellow here is a guess artist.

—A real guess artist? asked Piers Golp. I didn't know there were any left.

—I'm not like the others, said the guess artist.

—I didn't mean to intimate that you were, said Piers Golp. I only wanted to get across to you my pleasure at your choice of profession, and at the means we now have at our disposal for a fine and elegant conversation.

—You speak well, said S. I like a man who knows how to converse.

—Thank you, said Piers Golp. I once had the pleasure of speaking to the great Oscar Wilde. You know, he was the greatest conversationalist we have yet had among us. We as human beings, I mean.

—I have heard that said, said S. It seemed true then, and it seems true now.

The guess artist stood up and went to the window. He tried to pull up the shutter, but it was stuck fast and wouldn't move.

—Don't even bother, said Piers Golp.

720 —I think I will have that drink of water, said S.

He went over to the bust of Verlaine and pulled on the bell cord.

—Don't do that! exclaimed Piers Golp. He hopped out of the chair he was sitting in and went behind the table, ducking down behind it so that he could not be seen.

Far away across the house, a bell could be heard ringing. A great sound of shouting could be heard coming closer. S. looked at the guess artist with a question in his eyes. The guess artist returned the question to him unopened. At that moment, the door was thrown wide, and Caroline stood there, in a fury.

—Did someone call for the servant? she asked.

725 —Not me, said the guess artist. I was just standing here by the window.

Without making any examination of the room, Caroline called out,

—Was it you, Piers Golp? Did you ring the bell?

—Not me, Mrs. O'Shea. It wasn't me.

He came out from hiding and stood there fragilely holding his hands.

730 —I can smell him, you know, even when he hides, she said.

At this the old Mr. Golp shrank even more, and seemed on the verge of breaking.

—Leave him alone, said S. I'm the one who rang the bell.

—YOU RANG THE BELL? she shouted.

—That's right, he said. I rang the bell because I want some water. Now go and fetch it, on the double.

—Very good, sir, said Caroline, curtsying.

She left the room.

The guess artist and Piers Golp looked at each other in shock.

—Not bad, said the guess artist. But how are we to get out of here?

—I have an idea, said S.

He drew his map out of his sleeve again and looked at it a moment.

—The next bit is a little odd, he said.

—Anything has to be better than this, said the guess artist. No offense intended to you, Mr. Golp.

Piers Golp sank into a chair and nodded to indicate that he had taken no offense and also to indicate that he knew very well the undesirable nature of life at 14 Beard Street.

S. came over and knelt down by Piers Golp's chair.

—Haven't you something to say to us, Mr. Golp? he asked.

—Well, said Piers Golp, as a matter of fact, I do.

A tiny bit of light came from the out-of-doors around the edges of the shuttered and draped windows. It made its way slowly and carefully over to the three friends and settled on them.

—There is, said Piers Golp, in this city, a certain anonymous pamphleteer whose work I greatly admire.

He held up the book he had been reading. This turned out in fact not to be a book at all but a substantial pamphlet, neatly and elegantly folded to produce the illusion of a book if viewed from a distance of twelve to fifteen feet. On its cover it said: *An Inquiry into the Ultimate Utility of the Silly, as Prefigured in the Grave and Inhospitable.*

750 —Is this a particularly good one? asked the guess artist.

—I've only just begun it, said Piers Golp. My very favorite is one entitled, *Entering Rooms, a Grammar and Method.*

To all this S. said nothing, but only sat upon his heels, watching very carefully the tides and eddies of expression pass over the face of Piers Golp.

—About this pamphleteer, Golp continued, almost nothing is known. A friend of mine who knows about my predicament here sends me every pamphlet he can get his hands on. He knows how I long for news of the outside world. After all, I was for many years a war correspondent.

—A war correspondent, exclaimed the guess artist.

755 —Except that, said Piers Golp a bit ashamedly, there were no wars at the time, so I stayed home.

The guess artist and S. nodded in an understanding way.

—The first of these pamphlets appeared about two years ago, said Piers Golp. Then, about a year ago, new pamphlets began to appear with much greater frequency. Also, they were better printed, and displayed an obviously greater degree of attention and skill. About him I can hazard little, save that he is a young man of great leaps. He is very sly and is best pleased only when he surprises himself. I think that it is most certainly the case that the best artists are the best because they have in their hearts an infinite affection for the objects of the world.

In one of these pamphlets, *The Foreknowledge of Grief,* he plots out a rubric for creating a person to fall in love with.

First, he says, you have to go out into the world. This is not a simple matter of going outside one's door. No, that is simply going out. That's what one does when one is on the way to the store to buy a loaf of bread, some cheese, and a bottle of wine. When one goes out into the world, one is shedding preconceptions of past paths and ideas of past paths, and trying to move freely through an unsubstantiated and new geography.

So, one goes out into the world, and then 760
one wanders about.

The querist goes out into the world, and wanders about. Perhaps the day is a pleasant one. It has rained while he was still sleeping, and this rain brought with it an attendant coolness that remained after the rain had gone north or east with the wind. The streets are fresh as though a blanket of snow has fallen. Each square of pavement has yet to be trodden upon. All the weight of past footsteps has been lifted. Through it the young man walks, looking up at the tops of buildings and into the boughs of trees. How often in our progress we forget to look up! And how much there is to see. A bird takes off from a branch and lands upon another. His eyes trail this bird, follow the branch, then follow the trunk of the tree back down to the ground. A dog there is running past just at that moment. His eyes perch atop the dog's standing fur, and are shuttled back and forth along the street, far down and up to the dog's mistress, who, in a loose pair of trousers and a light jacket, is returning from a morning promenade. Her hair is unkempt and in a morning disarray. Her face is flushed with the pleasure of the day. The young man has approached her with his eyes, in the company of her dog, but he will go no farther himself. She and the dog move off through the streets, and the young man continues.

He remembers that the pleasure he has in morning comes in part from a time in childhood when he would leave school and wander through the quieted town. Shaded streets were lined with silent houses. The beds of lawns cried out to be lain in. And how then he would go up to the old cemetery on Cedar Hill and lie in the cool space between the graves and sleep while all around him was still, and while, to his great happiness and enduring pleasure, his fellow pupils were seated in rows in a classroom, learning lessons.

In the city too there is a girl. She is the appropriate girl. But she is still sleeping, having refused sleep for the better of the night, having gone along a path of streetlights until the streetlights themselves went out, and the paling horizon ushered her up to her door and into her small room.

It is for this girl that the young man is looking. Day after day he wakes in morning and goes searching for her. In his work, and in his life on mornings that are not miraculous and afternoons that are sundry and various, he saves the corners of his eyes for her, and watches at all times the entrances and exits of every establishment to which he comes.

For he knows that eventually, in time and given some protracted period of days, weeks, and months, he will come upon her, and know her in an instant for who she is.

He pauses sometimes in the rooms that he 765
keeps, looking over the equipment of his chosen profession, the printing press, the lithograph machine, the rolls of butcher paper, and endless space of desks and typewriters. He looks at the stacks of pamphlets he has made that are piled in corners and pinned upon the wall. And he thinks and knows in his heart that there is one glorious pamphlet waiting yet to be made. He calls this pamphlet by its name, *World's Fair 7 June 1978,* and he longs for its arrival. Somehow he knows it is tied to the girl he cannot find.

Oh, the *World's Fair*. What wonders will fill its pages? He makes notes towards its construction, building in his head and upon the page schematics of impossible architecture, pathways that stretch out across water, preserving in themselves a flatness of the earth to oppose every roundness, or a house in which all sound is diverted and played both upon and with, moved here and there, at distance and closeness, words sometimes amplified, sometimes dampened, and phrases cast upon precise winds, both proscribed and known.

He ponders interviews with artists who were never born, who say things he himself would like to say. These persons, beginning with a perfect biography, an inexplicable and wondrous origin, go on to thunder out the objects of his own hope. Oh, the *World's Fair.* If there is an affection, a complete and dear affection, it is to this idea of the book that he will one day write.

He stood by the door one day, trying to replicate a posture he had seen in a mannequin, when the door sounded with a loud knock.

—Who's there? he asked.

—Let me in, came the reply.

The pamphleteer went to the door and slowly opened it. A girl was standing there, dressed in the sort of khaki suit that best befits early-twentieth-century female explorers of Africa.

—Sif! he said. How nice to see you.

—And you, she said. It has been some time, I think.

—Yes, he said. I have been busy working on a pamphlet.

—Which one? she asked.

A glint came into her eye.

—Have you finished *World's Fair 7 June 1978*?

—Of course not, he said. This one is a method for how to enter rooms.

—Well, then, said Sif. Let this be a lesson to you.

She entered the room, doing a slow sort of pirouette.

—Will you get a girl a drink?

She sat down on the edge of the sofa and watched him as he brought out a glass bottle that perhaps had once held wine, but now looked very much like

—Iced tea? he asked.

—Yes, thank you, she said. You know, I was thinking about the story you told me the other day. The one about the gambler. I'm not entirely sure whether or not he was imagining the girl, what was her name, having affairs.

—Ilsa, said the pamphleteer.

—Yes, continued Sif. I think her dress was unbuttoned and her hair wasn't pinned up properly, etc., not by chance. I think it's very possible that a man who could disappear into, what was it, a fold of heat and light, could very easily appear in a room, ravage a woman, and then disappear.

—That's something to consider, said the pamphleteer.

—But on the other hand, said Sif, the story is interesting because it's also possible that he is just crazy, that he imagined the whole episode with the devil, and that he is imagining all her possible adulteries. I mean, the point of it could just be that it's ridiculous in the first place that she should be his property, that he should be able to barter her as an object in his possession in a wager with Satan. Am I wrong?

—Well, said the pamphleteer, there is the burn on his wrist. That's real.

—He could be imagining that too, said Sif. He's the only one who ever saw it.

—But the Chinese woman referred to it. And her grandmother too, said the pamphleteer. You can't just ignore their testimony.

—Sure I can, said Sif, tossing her hair. That means nothing, and you know it.

The two sat quietly, drinking their iced tea.

—Was there pinot noir in this bottle before the iced tea? asked Sif.

—Bingo, said the pamphleteer. Boy, you're good at that.

—Can't help it, said Sif. I just like wine. Next time you should try a young cabernet. I think that would contribute better to the taste of the iced tea.

—I'll put it under advisement.

—Oh, so did you hear about the guy who's down at Coney Island?

—No.

—The guess artist, there was a piece on him in the *Times*. Supposedly, he can guess what you're thinking in three tries.

—Most people think about a very limited number of things, said the pamphleteer. Especially when they're at the beach.

—No, you sap, said Sif. He can tell you *exactly* what you're thinking. I'm going to go down today and see. You want to come?

—I've got some things I have to take care of here, said the pamphleteer. But we're supposed to have supper later on. The Tunisian place on Third, right?

—Yeah, said Sif. Seven o'clock.

—I'll see you then.

Sif stood up, straightened her skirt, and, leaning over the pamphleteer, gave him a long and lingering kiss.

—That's so you remember me all day.

—Wow, said the pamphleteer. You need to leave right now.

—See you 'round, said Sif.

In a blur of Nordic grace and khaki, Sif disappeared out the door. The pamphleteer sat, and looked at the bottle of iced tea. Cabernet, he thought to himself. Cabernet next time.

Sif left the pamphleteer's building and hailed a taxi with a peculiar and effective gesture known only to her and the people to whom she had confided it. This gesture was so effective that with it one was able to steal taxis from people who were upstream. One can imagine how valuable a technique this was in the devil-may-care world of New York City.

She got into the taxi.

—Coney Island, she said, and step on it.

Out of her bag she took a booklike object. First there was a thin card-stock cover. *Entering Rooms, a Grammar and Method,* it said in neat black letters. Out of this cover, she slid the pamphlet of the same name. She opened it and began to read.

> Upon coming to a threshold one should always consider the possibility that there may be something hostile awaiting one within. Also, there may be some great pleasure, which, with its sudden and implacable onset of joy, may disarm one even more than the deepest hostility. Sometimes one must be more careful of being seen in happiness than in grief or anger. A great deal may be told from the expression of a happy man or woman. In any case, one must be prepared for the worst, and ready. Therefore, pause a moment before passing through a door, unless, of course, one is being watched on the outside, or one's approach to the door is being timed, as in a

situation when one is buzzed through an exterior door. In that case, one does not have the leisure to pause, for that pause would in its turn be noted and interpreted in a variety of ways, some of which would be harmful. Therefore, perhaps we should say, make the pause a mental pause, a sort of inner unveiling of precaution. It should last barely a second, and immediately preface the entering of the room in question.

Now, when one enters a room one should consider all the angles that are now present from which one's person may be approached. One should instantly scan the room, looking not with a particular gaze, but with a gaze in general. This second sort of gaze is a more comprehending gaze, and allows the faculty of the mind a greater freedom.

Gunfighters, when entering a hostile situation, have a vague eye that assesses the room at once with a piecemeal faculty, and at once in a coherent vein. They arrange in a flashing second the hierarchy of shooting ability on the part of every man, woman, and child there present. Thus when the gunfighter begins to shoot, killing the various inhabitants, he kills them not from right to left, or left to right, as we often see in films, but according to the prescriptions of his established hierarchy, from strongest to weakest. First he might shoot the old man half-hidden by the bar. He knows the old man was a captain in the Mexican cavalry and that, furthermore, there is a shotgun behind the bar that must not under any circumstances come into use. Then next he spins and takes out the wealthy rancher on the stairs. He has been guested several times at the ranch and knows the rancher's prowess with the silver-touched pistols he keeps at his side. These two gone, the gunfighter may continue, shooting down first the youngster with the Winchester, leaning against the faro table, and then and only then the cowboy on the near side of the bar. Now, you may say, why wait that long to shoot the cowboy? Alone among the people in the bar, the cowboy has two pistols, and one drawn already at the gunfighter's approach. Well, it is true that the cowboy may be able to get off two or even three shots before the gunfighter can attend to putting a bullet through his hardy skull. However, the gunfighter relies upon the fact that the cowboy is a terrible shot, this fact gleaned from the state of his pistols, which have obviously not been cleaned or attended to for some time.

So you can see, the proper method of entering a room has more to do with observation than with any particular grace or finesse. A girl who is a real knockout and carries herself with verve and élan must necessarily . . .

—Coney Island, said the cabbie. That'll be seventeen dollars.

Sif reached into her wallet, took out a twenty-dollar bill, folded it twice, and then handed it through the portal.

—I have to get my luggage out.

—All right, said the driver.

They got out of the cab and went around to the back. The cabdriver opened the trunk. Inside there was a birdcage with a canary in it. The birdcage was finely crafted, made from some exotic wood that matched in its texture the feathers of this rare canary.

—Did you put that in there? asked the cabdriver. I don't remember you putting that there.

—I called ahead, said Sif.

She took the birdcage out and walked up the steps to the boardwalk. It was a very sunny day and there were many people walking arm in arm. Damn that man, thought Sif to herself. This would have been such a fine day to be in love.

She observed in the distance a booth that

resembled the picture from the *Times,* and she walked in that direction. When she arrived, the booth did indeed say, GUESS ARTIST, but the man did not look like the man she had seen in the article.

Must be a copycat, she thought to herself, and continued down the boardwalk. After a few hundred yards, about six hot-dog stands, and nine crying babies, she came to the booth of the real guess artist. A very carefully old-fashioned man was speaking to the guess artist quietly.

It must be hot, thought Sif, in all that black clothing. But the man looked very happy standing there speaking to the guess artist. When the man was done and had left, Sif approached.

830 —And the Maccabean Revolt? she asked.

—A little, said the guess artist. But mostly we talk about the phenomenal calendars of the Aztec civilization. That man is an expert on calendars of all kinds. Probably the foremost calendar expert in the world.

—Does he have the one with the cats dressed up like people? asked Sif, who liked always to say things both carelessly and with a touch of sarcasm.

—No, he appreciates cats for what they are and hates it when their owners dress them up.

—Good, said Sif. I like him already. So, I brought you this.

835 She set the canary down on the counter.

—If you're right, you get the canary. If you're wrong, I go and give the canary to the fake guess artist down the block. She gave the guess artist a merciless look.

—But I get three tries, said the guess artist.

—Three tries, agreed Sif.

She lifted herself up onto the counter, crossed her legs, and leaned against one of the booth poles. Her eyes were very keen and sharp, and she fastened them on the guess artist's temples. Let's see how good he really is, she thought to herself.

The guess artist stood up and came around 840
the counter. He leaned against it and peered at her. She inclined her feet and let her sandals fall onto the boardwalk, one, two.

—If you think you're making it harder for me, you're not, said the guess artist.

—Stop stalling, said Sif. What am I thinking?

—You're thinking, said the guess artist, that this whole business of there being only seven days to the week is a big lie, and that there are actually eight, but that one is hidden, and that if you can discover it, your life is lengthened by that exact proportion, but better even than that, you get one day a week when only the people in the know are out and about, and it is on that day that all the best conversations happen.

—I think you're still stuck on that calendar expert, said Sif. I wasn't thinking anything like that at all.

—All right, said the guess artist. You're 845
thinking about the fact that the cage and its

canary were in the trunk of the cab by chance and that it was only by chance that you thought to tell the cabdriver to open the trunk and that you lied to him about it, and should you feel bad about lying to him? Because you don't, but you wonder if a regular person would.

—No, said Sif. Not me. Try again.

The guess artist gave her a searching look. He nodded to himself.

—You're thinking that the pamphleteer whom you are in love with maybe doesn't love you as much as you would like, and perhaps you should put some kind of truth serum into the Tunisian food at supper tonight so that you can ask him questions about what he does when you're not around.

—Geez, said Sif. You *are* the real guess artist. Do you know where I can get truth serum from?

850 —Sodium Pentothal? asked the guess artist. There's a Russian guy several blocks that way, on Avenue Y. He supposedly sells old Soviet army gear. He's the one to talk to.

He wrote the address of the store down on a piece of paper.

—Well, said Sif. Thanks.

—No problem, said the guess artist.

—One more thing, said Sif. You don't get the canary until you tell me what he's thinking. And don't lie, because I can tell when people are lying.

—I know that, said the guess artist. Give me a minute. 855

He looked intently at the canary. Then he reached out and rattled the cage a little. The canary leapt from one spot in the cage to another. The guess artist began to cry.

—Shit, said Sif. I was afraid that would happen.

—Don't worry about it, said the guess artist, wiping his face with a handkerchief. However, I refuse to tell you what he's thinking. It's too sad. Nothing so sad has ever been said out loud.

Sif shrugged her shoulders. She opened the cage and let the canary out. He flew up and landed on her shoulder.

—Later, she said. 860

—So long, said the guess artist.

Sif walked off down the boardwalk, canary clinging to her shoulder. The guess artist sat down behind his booth. What a day, he thought. Just then a kid ran up to the counter. It was the guess artist's apprentice, Gustav.

—Hey, Gustav, how are you? he asked.

—I'm all right, said Gustav. My frog died.

—That's too bad, said the guess artist. 865

Someone came up to the booth. A very heavy man with a large briefcase. The guess artist made a signal to Gustav to come around the counter.

—Hello, he said to the man.

—Hello, said the man. Quite a day.

—Yes, said the guess artist, a day for painting eyes onto the eyelids of the dead.

—I haven't heard anyone say that in a long time, said the heavy man. Anyway, can you guess what I'm thinking?

—I can, said the guess artist. And so can my apprentice here.

He pointed to Gustav and smiled proudly.

—But it takes him more tries. Do you have a minute? he continued.

—Sure, said the heavy man. Go on, then.

—By the way, said the guess artist, leaning over the counter and whispering: His frog just died, so take it easy on him.

—All right, said the heavy man.

Very quietly, then, to the guess artist, he said,

—I'll think of something historic.

He closed his eyes and then opened them.

—Go on, he said.

Gustav made little fists and hunched over. He growled a little bit like a dog and then straightened up. His eyes had gotten very big.

—It was in Russia, many years ago. Perhaps it was the reign of the empress Elizabeth. Her palace in Moscow was as grand a palace as had ever been, and all her courtiers were beautiful and elegant, and any one of them was wiser than the wisest man could ever be today. Now, Elizabeth was a virgin empress. She had never taken a lover, and once she came into her majority, she began to look around for an appropriate man upon whom to fasten. Before her gaze, then, the Count M.

M. was a renowned man. An accomplished horseman, a deadly duelist, a killer of bears, a tried soldier, and an excellent dramatist; whatever he turned his hand to flourished. He had been at court when the empress was a young girl. At that time he had gone away to make his reputation. Having made it he had returned, and she longed for him to think of her not as the girl she had been but as the woman she was. And so she lavished every reward she could on him. She gave him a great estate in the western marches; she gave him servants and a large house in the city. She brought her gifts to bear upon his friends and acquaintances. To those whom he showed favor, she showed favor. In short, the star of the Count M. rose as never any star had risen before.

And for these gifts of favor, all the count had to do was make attendance upon the empress, and bring her things that she desired. She loved, for instance, the tiny flowers that bloom only at dawn on the wayward side of hills that have not seen human step in six generations of man.

885 For these flowers he would hunt, on his splendid charger, galloping with his Cossack guard up and down the broad plains.

Her joy upon the reception of these little nothings was boundless, and she longed to throw herself into his arms. However, she was the empress and he a mere count. Things had to be done properly, and that would take time.

It was at this moment in the empress's reign that a certain grand duke came to court, and along with him his daughter. This girl was unremarkable in any way, save that for some reason, the count was riven by her, and could think of nothing else, could stir to no action but to go to the grand duke's house, day and night, and pay court to her hand. The girl was sensible of the great honor being done her, but was frightened by the possible anger of the empress. The affair was hushed up for a fortnight, but when it became obvious to all that the count no longer was coming to see the empress, all wondered where he was going instead. And in that time the Count M. was married to the daughter of the grand duke. So soon the truth came out.

The empress, needless to say, was pierced to the heart. She wept and cast herself repeatedly onto the ground in her opulent dressing chambers. She looked into the mirrors there surrounding her and could find no reason in her own appearance and grace, for there had rarely been a woman born in the world so lovely as the empress.

Then her sorrow turned to rage. She called to her ministers and convened a council of which it has been said no council ever bore so particularly upon a single hatred as this of the empress Elizabeth.

Her first act was to call to her first minister.

—Inovsky, she said. I want you to strip the Count M. of all his lands. I want you to strip him of all his honors. I want you to strip his family of their lands and honors. I want you to cause terrible things to happen even to people he vaguely regarded from afar with affection.

—Very good, said the Count Inovsky, who had long despaired of regaining the empress's ear in light of the dominance that the Count M. had recently enjoyed.

—Torvald, she called out.

—Yes, Empress, responded her second minister.

—I want you to have the marriage of the Count M. and the grand duke's daughter annulled. I want her to be married off again to the most brutal man you can find, perhaps that Italian ambassador, Balthazar something, whatever his name is.

—At once, my empress.

—Third Minister, she shouted.

Her third minister then came out from the dark, shaded portion of the room, where he had been standing quietly. The first two ministers were astonished to see him. They had not known he was still living, and they certainly had not thought he retained any of the power that he had once used to scourge the land in the reign of the empress's father. For the third minister was a dastardly and evil man, infamous for his depravity.

—Yes, my dear, he said, presuming even then upon her diabolical favor.

—I want you to search throughout our land of Russia. Search everywhere, in and out of borders, frontiers, estates. I want you to find for me the ugliest woman who now lives in our broad and implacable land. Bring her here.

—Thy will be done, said the third minister.

One week passed, then another. The Count M.'s life was ruined in a single blow. His wife was married off to another; his fortunes were dispelled with an imperial stamp. He tried even to kill himself, but was stopped by the first minister's soldiers, and kept under watch to await the empress's pleasure.

All up and down the land the third minister traveled in a dark coach, sampling the ugly wares of this burg and that hamlet. He traveled even into the depths of Siberia, along obscure trade routes to forgotten principalities. After two months he returned, and in his train was the ugliest woman that ever man had set eyes upon. He brought her in secret conference before the empress, and the smile that rose then upon her face would have lit a ballroom.

—We are pleased, she said. You do no disservice to your own twisted reputation.

—I thank you, he said, and did a manic little bow.

Meanwhile, the ugliest of women stood by, worrying at the sleeve of her shift.

—Where did you find her? asked the empress in the tone of voice a botanist might use in conversation with a colleague, a tone of clinical curiosity.

—In Szarthel, said the minister. She is the daughter of a wealthy merchant. For many years he kept her in his house, her only company the many books that lined the walls. One of my soldiers saw her through a window, and brought me word.

The empress nodded. Her lovely features tensed a moment in a paroxysm of cruel thought.

—Organize for me, my minister, said the empress, a parade of misshapen and frightening folk. Bring me dwarves and giants, beasts and patch-skinned dogs. Arrange for me a parade. For I mean to marry the Count M. to this our lady, and I mean to have a wedding party that the world shall remember.

Out then the minister went, and he gathered together the makings of this parade. As per the empress's plan, he commissioned the building of an ice palace at one end of Moscow. The parade was to begin at the other.

The day in question dawned slowly and silently. The empress went down in the dissipating darkness to the room where the ugliest of women was being kept.

—You, she said.

The ugliest of women said nothing.

915 —Today you are to marry the man whom I once loved. Do you know this?

Still the ugliest of women said nothing.

—I am giving to you possibly the most remarkable man that was ever born and raised in this our land of Russia. He is a king among men. His tastes are the most refined tastes, his passions the most refined passions. I am giving him to you, forcing you upon him, because I know how horrible it will be for him who was once raised above all other men to taste the wares of a creature as despicable as you. What do you have to say to that?

To that, the ugliest of women said nothing, and the empress went away. But there in the dawn, the ugliest of women smiled, and she said to herself, Still I will make him happy. Ugly as I am, I will please him, if he is so great a man.

The guard who had admitted the empress came then again to the ugliest of women.

920 —There is someone to see you, Kolya, he said.

—Thank you, said Kolya quietly. I would like that.

Then a young woman entered the room, dressed strangely. She sat down beside Kolya and took her hands into her own.

—This is how things are going to proceed.

And she told Kolya the remainder of the story. This heartened Kolya tremendously, and she thanked the girl, even going so far as to kiss her hand. The girl gave Kolya a drawing that looked like this:

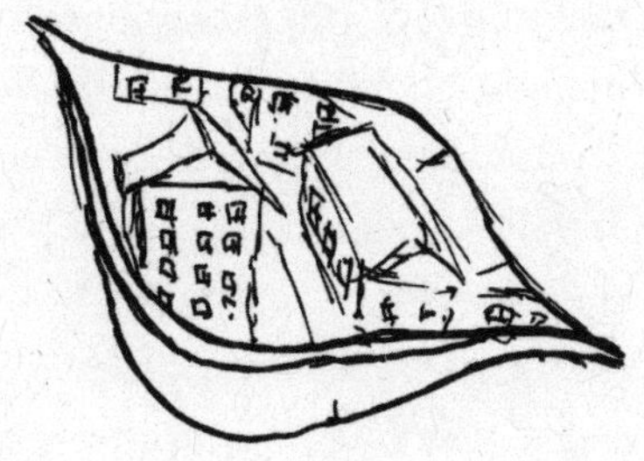

and then went away. The guard came soon after, with waiting women who bore Kolya's wedding gown. Bells rang out across Moscow. The populace was roused. All the major nobles were forced to be in attendance upon the empress for the spectacle that was about to unfold.

Out then into the street came the ugliest of 925
women, dressed in a gown so lovely that none who saw it could report ever having seen anything its equal. The empress was a brilliant general in this her war, and she had realized the glorious touch that a faultless gown would give to the proceedings. She had hired the best dressmakers in all of Russia, and even brought in an expert from France who was later strangled in a town near the border.

The ugliest of women stood defiant as the crowded street prodded her with jibes and the throwing of small stones. The empress had approved the throwing of stones no larger than a certain size. Such stones, she reasoned, would not harm the parade's participants, but might help in breaking their will. She had many stones of the precisely correct proportion distributed along the parade route in buckets stamped with her insignia. Such preparations she had made.

The ugliest of women waited, but not long, for after a moment a gate behind her was thrown open, and out of it poured the parade, gamboling on its hind legs, crawling and lurching, laughing and shrilling madly back and forth. But she did not stir from her expression, or tense a muscle towards flight. Quietly she turned her back upon the parade, and began to walk.

The empress was ahead, awaiting the coming of the parade, her court about her. And, tethered, as he had once tethered many a bear, the Count M. in rags, he too awaiting the coming of the parade. He did not know what was to happen, for he had been kept until this time in an oubliette beneath the empress's chamber. However, since emerging he had heard already six of the fifteen rumors that were circulating.

Up the boulevard, the ghastly parade! It rounded a slow curve and emerged into view. The Count M., seeing for the first time his fate, recoiled slightly. In his defense, perhaps he recoiled less at the horror of the features of the ugliest of women, and more at the lengths he suddenly saw that the empress had gone to in order to destroy him. By God, he thought. That woman must really have loved me. And for a moment he regretted having spurned her.

The empress's lovely breast meanwhile was heaving with pleasure and grand anticipation. She had seen the count twitch, and she had desired no more than that, had, in fact expected far less. For as we have said, the count was a redoubtable man, and not to be shaken easily.

The sound of bells as lepers ran around the edges of the pack. The rushing back and forth of the giants, trampling even into the crowd. The dwarves upon dwarves' shoulders, lighting fires and shouting the names of all the great wizards of the past. At their heels, the patchcoat dogs, and at the fore, the ugliest of women.

She approached the makeshift dais, and mounted one by one the stairs, prodded by soldiers with bills and halberds. Her dress was already filthy from the dwarves' Greek fire and the dirt of the street. She went before the empress and looked for the first time upon the Count M. He returned Kolya's gaze, held it gently in his own and did not look away.

For that I thank you, thought the ugliest of women.

Up then the priest onto the dais, elbowing his way through the throng. Shouts and cries abounded, and though it was winter, the heat of the press made sweat run down the hungry faces.

The count was untethered and forced to the side of his soon-bride. A stave brought them both to their knees, and as they fell, the count whispered in her ear,

—Pretend that you love me. I will do the same.

The ugliest woman nodded. To herself, she thought, You will love me yet, and not in jest.

The priest pronounced over them a joining, and to it they gave their agreement. The count and his new bride were raised then to their feet. The empress climbed onto horseback, with the members of her court. A great quantity of hounds was brought then into the streets.

—My count, called out the empress. And for the first time the count turned his eyes upon her.

—My count, she said, we will harry you through the streets as once you and I followed prey on the paths in the country of my youth. Do you see the palace in the distance?

Turning, the count beheld a palace of ice at the edge of the city.

—To that you must go. Raising a horn to her lips, the empress blew a loud clear note.

The count took the hand of the ugliest of women.

—Do not stumble, he said.

—I am ugly, she said, but I am quick.

And they were off.

It is lucky that they had the parade of dwarves and giants and patch-skinned dogs between them and the hunt, for otherwise they would not have reached the palace in safety. Yet as it was, the hounds took great pleasure in ravaging the lepers, who rang their bells for all they were worth, but did not fare so well in the hounds' sharp teeth.

Soon they were come, breathless and half-mad, to the ice palace. Rarely in the history of the great Russian Empire had such an ice palace been seen. A replica of the empress's own, this palace had in addition to many of the other rooms a bedroom set apart from the rest, with a bed constructed of ice, and a viewing chamber beyond.

As the Count M. stepped onto the threshold of the ice palace, the empress dismounted with her court. Soldiers once more took charge of the count and his bride. Together they were delivered to the bedchamber and made to stand fast by the bed of ice, facing the viewing chamber.

Into the viewing chamber, then, the court in general, and at its head the empress. All the nobles, the lords and ladies that the count had known, now looked upon him with a cruel and sneering eye. But what they saw in the count was nothing they had seen before. He looked back at them as though he were a man staring up into the night sky, with nothing more than idling and evening in his hand.

Out of a small door, then, the third minister. To the soldiers, he said,

—Off with their clothing. Force them onto the bed.

The count closed his eyes, then opened them. Without a word, he removed his own clothing and stood, naked, shivering only slightly from the deep cold.

For her part, the ugliest of women could not remove her dress on her own, for she had been sewn into it. With sharp knives the soldiers cut it off, and all of her was soon visible to the count's eye. He looked at her still and did not look away.

For this too I thank you, thought the ugliest of women. To him then she spoke.

—I am Kolya, she said.

—Think no more of the cold, Kolya, than of the audience, for they are the same. Here we will do what we must. If there is life beyond this, so be it.

The Count M. took Kolya to him then, and began to kiss her. In the viewing chamber the empress looked away. Tears started from her eyes, and she rushed from the room.

—Kolya, murmured the count. They lay upon the cold bed of ice, side by side. An hour had passed, and they were wrapped now in their rags and torn clothing. All the court had left, and all the soldiers too. They were alone, and had become inured to the ice.

—My count, said Kolya. My life has been till now a life of books. My father never took me out upon the street, to the marketplace or the promenade along the river. I never had schooling, or lessons on how to sew or cook. He kept me instead in his study and he told me, Learn all of this. Read every book and understand the things there writ. This will be your path to joy.

There was a book there, she continued, my favorite of them all. It constructed architectures, impossible places, dreams of impossible places. Of these a needle, larger than the tallest house, stabbed down into the sand at the sea's edge. It rises from the sand only enough for a single plank, a walkway, to run out from its center. This plank runs out across the sea, inches above the shuddering waves. It runs for miles, and a curious thing begins to happen as the walkway tends farther and farther from the shore.

—I have read this book, said the count. Beneath the plank, the sea begins to fall away, and the plank becomes steeper and steeper, and harder to climb. Miles pass in this way. Finally, there begin to be handholds, and footholds, ladder rungs in the plank. For one has come so far that one must climb. At the top, one finds that one has reached another needle, this sunk into an island so far offshore from the first needle that it was not visible, though from the top of the second needle the first needle is plain in the far distance, as the path's terminus.

—It is so lovely, said Kolya, how then there is another ladder, down along the side of the needle. One proceeds to the island of the anchored needle, where a small cabin sits, and someone is waiting with a bit of lunch and a pot of tea. Someone kind whom you have known a very long while. She comes to the door and plain upon her face is her joy at your arrival.

—You have come along the needle? said the count, in the voice of the someone-who-waits-in-the cabin. How long and tiring the route of needles, for it passes through the core of things.

965 —To this you say nothing, said Kolya, but only smile, admitting to the general truth of her words. And she brings you into the house and sets before you a fine meal. And afterwards, there is dancing and laughter, and it is the dancing one does when one is not observed, which is the best dancing of all.

—And all the while, said the count, someone murmuring, Who can say therefore where a certain person is, for what is it that anchors a person? Is it their place in the story to which you are a part? Many stories hereabouts run side by side, and you cannot be at pains to unpin them, for they are sharp, and you will only sting the tips of your fingers.

Their voices grew quiet, and they lay, staring up at the icy ceiling. The count ran his fingertips along the back of her neck, and a look of helplessness came over her face.

—The empress waş right about you, she said.

—No one has ever been right about you, said the count.

970 —Not yet, said Kolya. Not yet. But this is my debut.

The count began to say something about the events of the day, but Kolya put her hand over his mouth and stopped him.

—Today we will speak only of absurd and improbable things, things far from us.

The count nodded.

—Of absurd things, and of the *World's Fair 7 June 1978.* An impossible date, said the count. The world will have ended long before that.

—And a good thing too, said Kolya. There 975
is nothing so awful as a world that continues after it ought to have failed.

—I had a dream once, said the count, and as he drew in his breath to speak, it seemed the very air around him grew insubstantial, a dream in which I was visiting friends at a country estate. They were people I had never met in my true life; however, in this dream we were the best and oldest of friends. I arrived in some kind of mechanical apparatus, and was left by the gate, holding a sort of leather rucksack with my clothes and things. My friend's wife ran down to meet me from the house. She was wearing a thin cotton dress with a flowery print. I dropped the bag and caught her up in my arms. In the dream I remembered then a past in which she and I had been lovers, long ago, when we were young, and how all that was behind us, and there would be no more of it, but that it had been a glorious thing for us both, and still was, and that she was glad that I had come, and I was glad to have come, and it felt good to lift her up and feel her body against my own. We walked up to the house, talking of nothing, of small things, really, of cats and the distance of the sun. My friend came out into the doorway, tall, strong, a man of whom one says afterwards, I wish that he were here, for our troubles could be dealt with so easily. He embraced me too, and with him there was a sudden and long past, brought up like a bucket the size of a well out of a well the size of the sea. And how we had missed each other. How so many times I had resorted to remembering things he had said or done and how that had pleased me in my time. I was welcomed into their house and our holiday began.

They lived on a sort of vineyard, and in the first days they began to teach me how one keeps a vineyard, how one cares for the grapes, how certain fields lie fallow and others bear fruit. I learned about the shade of the porch in the long afternoon, where we would sit, drinking iced drinks from tall glasses, and watching the dogs sleep and wake and sleep again.

But something began to happen. There were other people present too, people who worked at the vineyard, as well as a few servants to see to the house. There was a sort of human drama always going on, with people entering rooms and leaving them. One man would stick his head in a window, another would emerge from a cellar. People were always conversing and talking about this or that. At some point I was walking, crossing a field beside my friend. He was dressed, I recall, in a linen shirt with deep brown pants, rolled up, and bare feet. His hair was unkempt, and his eyes had that incredible quality that eyes have that are blue and also long beneath the sun.

He began to speak to me on some subject, and I responded. Someone shouted something from across the field, and then I realized what had been lurking just beyond the edges of my comprehension: the things that people were saying to one another, the way that one action blended into another, the shifting times of day, and the pleasures of companionship, but most of all the dialogue: we were in a novel. There was no other explanation. No one spoke like this in ordinary life, picking up every inch of what had been said, and delivering it back with a twist and a nuance. It had not happened just once. I felt that each remark somehow carried with it the implication of all others previous. One felt very clearly a comprehending intelligence strung through the air, setting each new moment into motion. I wrested myself out of the necessity to do and say without decision, the leash that had accompanied my passage hitherto through the book that was all about me, and a further thought occurred to me: how could a person wander into a novel? It must be a dream. Then, realizing that I was in a dream, all became possible.

I said to my friend, This is a dream. And he looked at me blankly.

—That's ridiculous, he said. But funny. Imagine that! You, Robert, saying that this is all a dream with that dead serious expression on your face. I can't wait to tell Isabel. She'll laugh and laugh. Let's go back to the house and tell her.

He pulled on my arm, touching me with that tacit permission that is between the best of friends.

I looked at him sadly. For we had had such a fine time, but now it was all over.

—Good-bye, my friend. I'll miss you.

985 —I'll see you at dinner, he said, still smiling, unbelieving, and turned away, already crossing the field.

But I, I rose up straight into the air, and saw beneath me the vineyard spread out, and beyond that, unestablished country, unestablished for I had not yet flown over it and decided in my passage what might or might not exist, creating it even as I glanced in depth upon each thing in turn.

Yes, I was flying and dreaming and shooting through the air at blinding speed. The feeling is glorious, and better than anything in this world. But at some point the dream can again take hold, and one forgets that one is dreaming. One stumbles, and again is bound to the dictates of something half created, half imagined.

—You see! he said, striking his hand upon his knee. That's the difficulty. Things must be done easily and well or not at all. For instance, in the city even now a young man has entered the Seventh Ministry building. It is a fine and beautiful day in the fall. Fall is, of course, the best season in that city of cities.

The air is crisp and the leaves on the trees

that line the streets have begun to change. As he crosses the doorstep and passes within, he sees behind the desk dear Rita the message-girl.

—Rita, he says.

—Selah! We haven't seen you in quite some time.

—Any messages?

Rita pushes down an intercom button on her desk.

—He's back, she says into a tiny microphone hidden in the flower vase. He looks a bit skinny, but otherwise no worse for wear.

—I was working, he replies. I heard a story, a good one: There was a municipal inspector who, on a day in October, returned to his work after some time away. He entered the building and saw his dear old friend Rita the message-girl. She was pleased very much to see him and reported his presence to the chief inspector. Afterwards, he took her hand and they did a minuet all around the room.

Rita stands, offers her hand to the young inspector. He takes it and they do a minuet all around the room. Rita is looking especially beautiful on that day, and the young inspector has the urge to kiss her. However he does not, because he likes the way things are at the ministry and does not want them to change.

Into the room then, comes the chief inspector, Levkin.

—Selah, he says. Come here. I have something to show you.

Selah goes with him, spinning Rita once more into and out of his embrace. In the next room, Levkin has set up a 16mm film projector and a screen. He goes along the windowed wall, untying the drapes. The room becomes dark.

1000 —Sit, he says.

Selah sits down in a large leather chair, and Levkin switches on the projector. The film reel begins to turn, and light is thrown onto the screen. Numbers running, and then brilliant sunlight. A woman, regally dressed, a queen of some kind, entering a guarded room. She is extraordinarily perfect in every way, her chin, her nose, her eyes, her throat, the manner of her walking, standing, the motion of her wrists. Selah watches, hushed.

The door is opened by a guard, and the queen is admitted. In the room, seated by a small window, is a grotesque figure. A woman whose features are unpleasant, yes, difficult to look upon. The queen says to her,

—You.

The other says nothing.

1005 —Today you are to marry the man whom I once loved. Do you know this?

Still the other says nothing.

—I am giving to you possibly the most remarkable man that was ever born and raised in this our land of Russia. He is a king among men. His tastes are the most refined tastes, his passions the most refined passions. I am giving him to you, forcing you upon him, because I know how horrible it will be for him who was once raised above all other men to taste the wares of a creature as despicable as you. What do you have to say to that?

To that, the ugly woman continues to say nothing, and the queen goes away. The light pouring through the window has the sheen of new light, of early light bred away in the east and brought here with a spring in its step. It dances through the window, coming in turn upon the face of the wretched woman and the queen, and delighting in both.

And there in the dawn, the ugly woman smiles.

—Still I will make him happy. Ugly as I am, 1010
I will please him, if he is so great a man.

The film reel blurs for a second. It is in black-and-white, and very grainy. The guard is speaking. His voice is distorted.

—There is someone to see you, Kolya.

—Thank you, she answers. I would like that.

Then a young woman enters the room, dressed in a sort of flapper outfit. She sits down beside Kolya and takes her hands into her own.

—THAT'S HER! shouts Selah and jumps 1015
to his feet. MORA KLEIN!

—I thought it might be, says Levkin quietly.

—This is how things are going to proceed, says Mora Klein to Kolya.

And bending, she whispers something into Kolya's ear. The film ends, and behind Selah the reel flaps against the projector.

—It was her, he says again. But how?

1020 —We are not certain, says Levkin, of whether that is: a. actual footage taken from the memory of someone who has not been delivered of the facts of their past life, b. a film shot in the 1950s, or c. a postulation on the part of a cruel and uncertain fate.

—I don't entirely understand, says Selah. What do you mean?

—Well, says Levkin. Your girl, Mora. She might have been in the event in question. Or she may have been in the original historical occurrence. Therefore, should this prove a filmed reconstruction of the historical occurrence, they would then have had someone playing her with greater or lesser skill. Perhaps enough skill to fool you into thinking you are watching her.

—But, says Selah.

—Or, continues Levkin, she somehow managed to be present both in the historical scene and in its reconstruction and subsequent filming.

1025 —I begin to see, says Selah. I will have to think about this.

Both men stand and look at each other in the darkened room.

—So you've been working on pamphlets? asks Levkin.

—I've finished it, says Selah.

—What have you finished?

1030 —*World's Fair 7 June 1978.* It is my precondition, set at the start of the world.

—Very good, says Levkin. I will have to

look at it. I thought, he says, that I saw someone a few days ago carrying a copy. I tried to look closer, but she noticed me watching and hurried away.

—Sif, says Selah. A girl. She came to the apartment of the pamphleteer.

—The pamphleteer? asks Levkin.

—The pamphleteer, replies Selah.

Levkin nods in a Levkin-like-Wednesday- 1035
way. Selah continues.

—Selah, she said, I want very much to read your WORLD'S FAIR and I am not about to wait any longer. She was wearing a short dress with very spectacular Roman legionnaire sandals that strap all the way up to the knee.

The pamphleteer had just come from a bath and was wearing a flannel nightshirt.

—How did you get in? he asked.

—Your keys, she said, holding them up.

—I never gave you my keys. 1040

—But I spoke to your super and had copies made. I thought it would be prudent. I knew there would be a time when I would want to enter your apartment without your permission, and now that time has come. Give me the WORLD'S FAIR.

—But it's not done, he said.

—It will never be done, said Sif.

She came closer and grabbed his ear. The gesture was very rapidly done, and it flashed in the pamphleteer's head that he would like very much to draw a schematic of the action and put it in the *World's Fair 7 June 1978,* along with vector lines of force and angles of incidence, etc.

1045 —Here's the story, she said. I'm more stubborn than you are. I'm telling you now I won't let go of your ear until you let me read WORLD'S FAIR.

She gave him then her winningest smile.

The pamphleteer smiled too.

—You know, he said, I was thinking of taking all the smiling out of *W.F.* In *Seymour, an Introduction,* he goes on about how smiling is just awful and no one should do it, in books, at least. What do you think?

—Smiling is for the birds, said Sif. Now give me the goddamned book.

1050 —All right, said the pamphleteer. I'll give you an early version. But hold on a moment, because I have to add one more bit.

He walked over to his drafting table. On the butcher paper he quickly sketched out the schematic he had just imagined, complete with a figure indicating Sif and a figure indicating himself.

Sif (still holding on to the pamphleteer's ear), said,

—Do I really look like that?

—Much cuter, he said. And craftier-looking.

—Do I look crafty? she asked. 1055

—You're just the craftiest, said the pamphleteer.

This pleased Sif immediately. The pamphleteer rose and crossed the room, Sif hanging on all the while. He proceeded to make a lithograph plate of his schematic. This took some time.

—Can I get a drink? asked Sif. I'm very thirsty.

—All right, just give me a second, said the pamphleteer. He put the plate into the lithograph machine, put some good-quality paper underneath, and made a print. Taking it out, he smiled.

—Not bad, said Sif. Now, to the refrigera- 1060
tor.

They crossed the apartment. Sif took a bottle of iced tea out of the refrigerator. She poured two glasses and returned it. Lifting the glass to her lips, she took a long sip.

With a spluttering laugh, she shook her head and put the glass down.

—Not an American cabernet, she said, an Italian, even a Chilean. American cabernets are fine. But not for this. . . .

She shook her head again.

—You really don't have the right instincts 1065
for this business of putting iced tea into old wine bottles.

—Fine, said the pamphleteer, blushing. Let's finish this so you can let go of my goddamned ear.

Together they managed a sort of three-legged race over to the printing press. The pamphleteer took a little box from off the top of a pile of little boxes. On the cover it said,

WF 7 J 1978

Out of the box he slid a thick pamphlet. He took the printed schematic sheet and, taking a sewing needle and some thread from off a table, sewed it into the pamphlet. Then, turning, he returned the pamphlet to its box, kissed it once upon its cover, and presented it to Sif.

—For you, he said. You'll be the first to see it.

Sif let go of his ear and did a little dance.

1070 —I'm so happy, she said. This had better be good. You've refused countless outings with a certain girl named Sif on account of you were working on an important book. SO it had better be good.

She threw her arms around his neck and kissed him. Then she danced off to the door. She pulled her bag off a hook on the wall, slipped *W.F.* into it, and herself slipped out the door.

—GOOD-BYE, she said. I'll be back soon.

—When? called the pamphleteer.

Sif's pretty head poked back through the door.

1075 —By good, I mean that the book had better make life better in at least six or seven definite ways immediately. Also, there had better be somewhere in it a method for handling fortune and chance so as to best provoke the most complicated, involved, and glorious refractions of what's possible.

—Look in section three, said the pamphleteer.

But Sif was already gone away down to the street. A man was passing, carefully transporting his entire life and a mustache with great speed between the tables, chairs, waiters, and regulars of a sprawling street café. She followed. This was how she chose her routes, by tailing someone for precisely seven minutes, deciding upon where he or she must be going, and then going there, independent of him or her. This course of action had often resulted in her arriving at a person's destination ahead of that person, which then gave that person the feeling that there were some favorable circumstances or kismet involving the two of them. But, in fact, it was merely caprice on the part of Sif.

At some point she entered a park and climbed a tree. Someone saw and told a policeman. The policeman came over. Sif was seated quite high up in the tree and was reading *W.F.* The policeman shouted up to her.

—Miss, he said, you'll have to come down.

She set her book a moment upon her 1080
crossed legs and peered down at the police officer. Taking from her bag a small square of card stock, she dropped it expertly. The card stock fluttered through the air and hovered a moment before the police officer, who caught it. It said:

Pardon me, I am almost entirely deaf. I would, in general, prefer not to speak to you, however, if you must speak with me, please write your remarks out legibly in longhand (or preferably type them), and deliver them to me. Two things: Do not use scraps of odd paper or the backs of promotional materials, envelopes, etc., for this purpose. I choose to read only elegantly assembled correspondence. And second, allow a period of time for me to read and then respond to your message. Also, I would appreciate if, during that time, you would go away. Find something else to do and then return. If you allow enough time I will be likely to have responded. I'm sorry that these measures are required of you, and also of myself, however, I am, as I have said, rather hard of hearing, and it would be kind of you to do this little thing in order to make me more comfortable in the world.

The policeman was young. He was a good-natured fellow and well liked. Everyone thought that he would go far. Already proposals were being put forward at the station house by his superiors that he ought to be transferred to Homicide and made a detective. He had the peculiar faculty of having the proper resources to deal with many odd and inflammable situations.

He read the card over twice, then put it into the pocket of his jacket. He looked up at Sif, met her gaze, then held up one finger. He walked away from her tree, left the park, and crossed the street. A copy shop was there. The policeman talked awhile with the clerk in the copy shop. The clerk immediately went into the back and attended to the policeman's order, putting it ahead of all the other orders that had piled up through the course of the day. Some few moments later he returned and pressed a package into the policeman's waiting hand. The officer thanked the clerk and left the store. He then went into the next store, which was a tobacco store. There he purchased an expensive Italian pen along with a bottle of ink. These in tow, he crossed the street, reentered the park, and took a seat at one of several stone tables. Sif's view of these stone tables was obscured, and though she had seen the other proceedings, she could no longer see what was passing. After perhaps five minutes, the officer reappeared beneath her tree. A small boy was with him. The officer handed the small boy an envelope. The boy shimmied up the tree to Sif. They looked at each other.

—Hello, he said. My name's Morris. I'm very good at walking far and at climbing trees.

—Do you have something for me? asked Sif.

—I do, said Morris the tree climber and far walker. He handed Sif an envelope. It was a printed envelope, and said,

---

Miles Lutheran
Officer of the Law
Tompkins Square Park Task Force

12 October xxxx
GIRL in TREE
Vocation or Title Unknown
Tompkins Square Park
Third Tree from the Street, within Fenced Enclosure Opposite East 340 Tenth Street.

Sif smiled to herself.

—Thank you, Morris, she said. You can go now.

—All right, said Morris, who proceeded to descend the tree very rapidly, going headfirst like a squirrel, but without difficulty or incident.

Sif opened the letter. She admired the penmanship and the quality of the ink and paper.

Dear Girl in Tree,

I'm sorry, but I am going to have to ask you to come down. This is principally because I am afraid for your safety, not because you are hard of hearing, but because it is a simple and easy thing to fall from a tree and hurt oneself. Now, I know that you don't think you are going to fall. You may say to yourself, I have never fallen. Why should I fall? Well, miss, falls are almost always unexpected.

Please come down. If you need a ladder, hold up two fingers and I will go about getting one. Otherwise, have a fine day.

Yours Most Sincerely and Assiduously,

Miles Lutheran

Officer of the Law

Sif put the letter back into its envelope. She took *W.F.* from off her lap and replaced it in its box. She then put envelope and box into her bag and climbed down from the tree. The policeman and boy were gone.

She walked very briskly up and down in 1095
front of the tree three times, and then went to sit in a little unmarked Thai bistro that took up all three floors of a brownstone on a nearby street. There was nothing on the exterior of the restaurant to let anyone know that such a fine and splendid establishment was within. Luckily, enough people knew about it that its existence was not in jeopardy. She took a seat near the back. After a moment a waitress appeared. This waitress crossed the floor slowly, not looking at Sif. At the

last moment, it was as though she looked up into Sif's face. She shouted out, SIF! and, untying her apron, pulled a chair up beside her.

—Dear Sif, she said. How nice of you to come.

—Shall we exchange confidences? asked Sif.

—Let's, said the girl.

Her name was Claude, just like the Maude.

1100 —He gave me the *W.F.,* said Sif. Want to see?

—It was no dream; I lay broad waking, said Claude.

—What? asked Sif.

—Where is it? asked Claude.

—Here, said Sif. She took the little box out of the bag, slid the *W.F.* out of the box, and handed it to the waitress.

1105 —How nice! said Claude, feeling with her hands the thin, expensive paper. Does it say, Since in a net I seek to hold the wind?

—I'll read it to you, said Sif. For though I am not deaf, it is after all true that you cannot see ordinary things like letters and books.

—Not letters or books or tables and chairs. Everything has to be precisely in the right place for me, said Claude. But this restaurant is a special place. I can find my way around here.

—Here, said Sif, you are the best waitress there has ever been.

—I know that, said Claude. There's no need for you to say it.

—I'm not saying it for your benefit, said Sif. 1110
I just like to say things that are true.

Claude snorted.

—You? Say things that are true? Why, you're the biggest liar ever to go uncaught! But as for me, alas, I may no more.

—That's not true, said Sif. You lie too. And Selah catches me all the time. I like to let him catch me lying. It's a game we play.

She picked up the *W.F.* from out of Claude's hands and opened it.

—The true gambler resorts only to gam- 1115
bling when all other avenues have failed. In this he gambles not so much on his own future as on the futures of others. His actions are irrelevant insomuch as his choice is not to include himself but to absent himself from proceedings in order to lend clarity to the parade of events.

Claude nodded.

—I have a machine at home that my parents bought for me, she said. It is a combination of sound, smell, and touch that is supposed to simulate the act of sight. I have never used it, though. I wonder if it works.

—Was it expensive? asked Sif.

—Very, said Claude. It costs the same amount as an expensive college education.

—Your parents must have been hopeful that 1120
you would use it, said Sif, if it cost that much.

—No, said Claude. The point is that, now that I have that device, if I want to see, I can. It changes my blindness from an undismissable fact and makes it a sort of choice. Like the gambler. You know?

—Oh, yeah, said Sif. I guess so. Do you think I could try that thing out sometime?

—What are you talking about? said Claude. I was lying. There's no device like that. You couldn't tell I was lying?

She smirked and caught up one of Sif's hands in her own.

1125 —I'm glad you came by, she said. I have to get back to work, but I will stop by your table in an official capacity several times, and then return to speak to you privately again before the end.

—Okay, said Sif.

—By the way, said Claude, that book is pretty swell. It into my face presseth with bold pretense.

—Thanks, said Sif. I like it too.

Claude jumped up onto her feet, replaced the chair at its table nearby, tied on her apron, spun about, and approached Sif's table again.

1130 —Good afternoon, she said. Her face was now entirely composed and businesslike.

—Hello, said Sif.

—Have you had a chance to look at the menu? asked the waitress.

—Yes, said Sif. I would like a Thai iced coffee, and the spicy noodle with chicken. Please make the spicy noodle very spicy. Tell the cook I want it as spicy as he himself would like to have it.

—Very good, said the waitress. I'll go put in your order.

Sif looked down at the book in her hands. She traced the cover with her fingertips and smiled. It was such an awfully nice-looking book. She reached into her bag and took out the policeman's letter. What a swell boy, she thought. I hope he is put in charge of the whole city one day.

In her head then, a play began.

Two actors dressed as birds wore harnessed costumes that allowed them to flutter here and there throughout a high-ceilinged theater. Their voices were very loud and bright and delightful to listen to. In the theater there sat only Sif and Morris the far walker and tree climber. Morris was up front and very engaged. One could see that already he had made up his mind to grow up as fast as possible so that he too could be a bird flying around on a cable in a theater.

The more brightly plumed bird said something incomprehensible to the dark-plumed bird, and the dark-plumed bird darkened like an evening sky. He took off and flew to the farthest part of the theater. Thus began an aside on the part of the light-plumed bird.

—There was a woman, he said, whose husband was a gambler. They lived deep in the countryside, deep in a deep countryside, at such a depth that descending into it and returning from it took a very long time. Sadly, there was in this place no possibility of the gambler making a fortune, or continuing a fortune already held, and so periodically he was forced to leave the side of his wife and go off to a nearby city to gamble and procure for them the money that they needed to live.

1140 And so, the gambler would go away for days on end, and leave his wife alone. At first there was no difficulty in this. She was a bright and clever girl and filled her time walking the woods of their small estate, discovering here and there in the country small things that she would tell the gambler of upon his return. And so for some time his absences did not pain or trouble her, for she acted and felt as though he were beside her, and when she went dancing through a stream on a wild and sunny afternoon with her skirt pulled up above her knees, she felt that he danced there beside her, and she was glad. And indeed when he was returned from any one of his trips, he would be dancing there beside her, and moving about at her side throughout the panoply of glittering incidents that well befitted their life together.

However, his trips continued to punctuate their life, and when he was away, a difficult thing began to happen. The woman, Ilsa, began to dream of a man in a green coat, a merchant. She dreamed of him while the gambler was away, and she dreamed of him when the gambler returned, and when the gambler went away again, and stayed away a week, the green-coated man rode up the path to Ilsa's house. From that moment on her life was torn in two. When the gambler was home, she was as she had been, the gambler's woman. But when he was away, even so far away as in another room, or on some other part of the property, she was the merchant's woman, and she felt his hands upon her.

Forever the merchant would be bringing her things, gifts, jewels, dresses, and Ilsa would have to hide them to keep them from the gambler's sight. She could not get rid of them, however, for the merchant demanded that she wear the dresses when he was present, that she have on display the tokens of his love. In the gambler's absence she constructed throughout the house secret places for belongings until almost all the walls were riddled with these secrets, with the gifts that the merchant had brought. In her dreams the merchant had been one man, always the same, and he had been that man when he first arrived, riding up the path. However, as time passed, many men seemed to her to be the merchant, and they would come to her as she lay abed, or as she walked through the rooms of her house, or about the edges of her land. When they did she gave of herself freely, and took of them what they would, and it hurt her only when she thought of the gambler and how he loved her. But already the man she had married was changing. He suspected somehow, though he never could have known, the things that she was doing. He would burst in upon her as she was in the midst of sleeping with an unknown man. She would be upon her back, naked and crying out, and the door would burst open, revealing the gambler.

At which point, strangely enough, as though

she were protected by some power, she would be removed already in a moment to the chair by the window, her dress done up and some bit of sewing placed into her lap. The man would be gone, and there would be only the gambler's rage, and her sudden fear and confusion.

Events continued, and her husband's fits of rage grew, until the two parts of her tore wholly the one from the other, and she no longer loved her gambler husband, for he had gone away entirely, replaced by this pale, ruinous man who himself had been ruined by the fates he had once held so easily in his hand. It was at this time that she fled their home, leaving in the company of a girl she had met upon the road, a strange girl who told her a story that made her heart light for a moment.

1145 It was the first time in what seemed like years that Ilsa's heart had been light, and so she treasured the girl and took seriously all that she said. The girl said,

—Come with me to the inn in Som. There are few places left where you may be safe. But that is one.

And she wept and said to the girl that she was terrified, and no longer understood herself or even such facts as the brevity of life (for to her life now seemed stretched and distended, a creature that would linger and linger on long past all sufferance). To which the girl said:

—Nonsense, Ilsa. Nonsense, or the truth. It is no matter. Come along. We have no need even of your things. There are things enough where we are going.

And they fled together down the road.

When they arrived at the inn in Som there 1150
was a tall black-bearded man awaiting them, and he told them to go upstairs to a certain room, and they knew that beneath his hand they would be sheltered from the green dream of the merchant that had so twisted her life.

—Go upstairs, said he, and I will attend to the rest.

Ilsa began up the stairs, and the girl along with her, but the bearded man called out,

—Mora, stay a moment. I would speak with you.

She came back down the steps to hear what he would say.

—You have gone very far from yourself, 1155
wandering in these dissipate geographies.

—I cannot tell one hand from the other, said Mora. I do not remember who I am, but only what I must do.

—That is as it should be, said the bearded man. But you shall learn more of yourself in time. Someone is looking for you, even now.

—If he should come here, said Mora, do not admit him until he has come thrice, and by three different paths. No matter what he brings me, or how hard has been his passage.

—This was my thought too, said the bearded man, and you have shared in it. It will be so. The tale is never forward, but always roundabout. Your young man must crowd the avenues in his search, and learn to cut doors through pages, through thoughts and guesses.

1160 Mora's face was sad, for she was afraid that he would never come, but she mounted the stairs then and went to the comfort of the gambler's wife, and the bearded man returned to the common room. A large dog was walking about on hind legs and playing the fiddle. The bearded man began to laugh.

—None of your business, now, he said. You of all present since the beginning shall not be allowed upstairs.

—Then tell me some news, said the dog, playing a neat little jig, and giving a good show with his feet.

—News, asked the bearded man, of what?

—Of the search for Mora, said the dog. I was listening while you spoke to her upon the stairs.

1165 —The search for Mora . . . murmured the black-bearded man to himself. I do not have news to tell.

Just at that moment, a young man burst through the door, brandishing a bat. He was wearing a very finely tailored gray-blue suit.

—Where is she! he snarled.

—That's the spirit, said the dog, and played a long wailing note on his fiddle.

—Enough of that, said the black-bearded man. Selah Morse! Leave the bat by the door and come sit down. There is much still to be told.

Selah tossed the bat back the way he had 1170
come. It flipped in the air, bounced, righted itself, and settled upright into a corner. Selah did not look back at it.

—Not bad, said the dog.

—You can't go upstairs, you know, the black-bearded man told Selah. She isn't ready to see you yet. You can't find her here until you've found her somewhere else first.

At this, the dog jumped up and began to caper about, for he had never before heard the black-bearded man tell a lie.

—Sit down, said the black-bearded man crossly. We can't have you capering about all the time. Now, Selah, tell us where you have been.

Selah leaned back and took a sip of the 1175
black-bearded man's pint of ale, which had been offered him a moment before.

—I'm afraid, he said, I promised not to speak of it. However, there are others who are not thus bound.

He called out in Russian, and after a moment another man entered and took his seat beside Selah.

—This, said Selah, is the guess artist.

The dog did a pretty bow and sat again. The black-bearded man inclined his head.

—We are all old friends, he said. Are we 1180
not?

—These two, said the guess artist, have plagued me from the first.

But he said it in a kind way.

—What shall I do with this? he asked, taking from his coat the polished skull of a cat.

Selah picked it up and handed it to the black-bearded man.

1185 —It is this, he said, that we have brought to barter for our passage upstairs.

The black-bearded man threw back his head, and his laughter shook the inn. The dog jumped up onto the table, upsetting the drinks, and broke the violin in two over his own knee.

—Never in my life, he said, have I seen such a perfect passage paid.

—But it will do no good, said the black-bearded man.

—Tell them how we came, said Selah to the guess artist.

1190 —By the forest route, said the guess artist. There was a storm in the caverns, and the sea had taken to wearing petticoats and bartering like a bandit with the ships that sought to pass across. We wanted nothing to do with that sort of trouble.

—Really tell them how we came, said Selah.

—But do you know to whom you're speaking? asked the guess artist.

—I am aware, said Selah. Nonetheless . . .

—Then there should be no need, said the guess artist.

1195 —And yet, said the dog, we too are limited by events.

—Then I should say, said the guess artist, that it was a bright and angry morning when the sailmaker looked up in his loft to see the guess artist and municipal inspector making their way towards him in great haste. The municipal inspector was holding a sheet of paper covered in scrawled crayon, and nodding with certainty to the guess artist. It seemed to be some kind of map.

The sailmaker had been sewing all night, and his hands were large and swollen from the effort of his work. His needles were very sharp and very long, and he stitched stronger and faster and more steadily than any man before or since, yet even he, after his long labor, was tired, and thought now only of his bed, and no longer of the ship that would soon be making its way across the skin of the water, having as *its* strength only whatever his own will might bestow.

—Sir, said the municipal inspector. He approached the man as one might some wary animal that moves very rapidly with only death in reply.

The sailmaker looked them up and down. By this we mean that he did not like what he saw.

—This reminds me, said he, of a short story 1200
called *The Arcadist.* There was a man, a stonemason, in that book who never wanted to be disturbed, and yet everyone was always disturbing him, and so in his town he built a sort of zocalo or center, with the most beautiful arcades that anyone had ever seen. Except that they were poisoned. It never said how, but people would go into the arcades and simply be gone. It was something to do with the color of the stone and the hour of day. At least, that's the sense I got.

—We are looking for a way to get upstairs, said the municipal inspector. It is widely thought that you are the wisest man who still consents to talk.

—I do consent, don't I? said the sailmaker-who-wished-he-were-an-*arcadist*.

—Certainly, said the guess artist.

—Fortunately, said the municipal inspector.

1205 —If I tell you where to go, then what do I get out of it? asked the sailmaker. I have been sewing this sail all of yesterday through to today. Now you come and ask for more work out of me. You will have to pay dearly.

To the municipal inspector the sailmaker resembled the hibernating bear of Eskimo legend that tells all the secrets of the world while still in its behusked sleep.

—I will give you something of equal value, said the municipal inspector. I can be trusted, he said with a curt nod. I am a municipal inspector.

—Are you now? asked the sailmaker with a disbelieving look. I thought there was only one. An older man.

—Once there was only Levkin, said the guess artist. Now there is Levkin and also M. Selah Morse.

1210 —Oh, you are Selah Morse, said the sailmaker. I have heard of you. You get around.

At that moment everyone turned and looked out an enormous window that stood just to their left. Something huge was moving rapidly across the sky. It was an old Victorian house, shuttling in and out of the clouds.

—It was true, then, said the municipal inspector.

—It is all true, said the guess artist and the sailmaker, each to himself. None of them heard the others.

After a minute, the Victorian house had gone so far west that it was no longer visible. The sailmaker spoke.

—If you want to get upstairs it is very diffi- 1215
cult, but not entirely impossible. You have to go first, here in our city, to the tallest building.

—The Empire State Building? asked the guess artist.

—No, said the sailmaker. This is another building, much taller than that. It has long been the tallest, but no one has ever known it, because it is in a very deep hole.

—Oh, said the municipal inspector. How nice.

—It is under the Manhattan Bridge, continued the sailmaker. No. Six Quince Street. A man will be sitting outside. Say virtually anything to him in Cantonese and he will let you by.

—I don't speak Cantonese, said Selah to the 1220
guess artist. Do you?

—No, said the guess artist, but if he is saying something to himself in his head, then I can guess it.

Both men nodded to each other. They

turned back to the sailmaker, who was still paused, needle in hand. It was a very long, very thick, and very sharp needle. The sort of needle that might be used to sew your heart shut with rope. Then the thought, What would they pay him? To this end, the municipal inspector spoke.

—I have in mind your payment.

—And a good thing too, said the sailmaker. Excuse me.

1225 He went into a little room behind a wall. For five minutes he was gone, and all that could be heard was the distinct clacking of the second hand of a clock upon the wall. Selah was deep in thought. The guess artist was attempting to figure out what Selah intended to do as payment.

—You are intending, he said, to leave me here as the sailmaker's indentured servant. I would live for five years and then die of tar poisoning, because the sailmaker's sails are poisonous and kill everyone who stays too long at their side.

—The sails aren't poisonous, said Selah. He only wants them to be. And no, you're too important in helping me to search for me to leave you here as someone's indentured servant. Besides, this poor man just wants to be alone. And you can't even make a decent pot of tea. Who wants an indentured servant who can't make a pot of tea? And furthermore, only struggling families in old books sell their children as indentured servants. The proper documents for such a transaction don't even exist anymore. And you know as well as I that such men as the sailmaker and myself only do things the proper way.

For the first time the guess artist lowered his head sadly, ashamed at the poorness of his guess. Selah felt chastened by his sadness.

—I'm sorry, he said. Perhaps I was a little curt. Your guesses are always either correct or worth listening to, and mostly both.

The guess artist brightened up. Out of the other room then came the sailmaker carrying three little cups brimming with some odd Romanian aperitif.

—Drink up, he said.

They all downed it in one go.

—Here is your payment, said Selah.

He stretched his shoulders, stretched his wrists, and then delivered himself of the following verse as payment in trade.

Birds that talk as men do
and make of their lives a human mess
drown quickly in the shallow pools
I'll see to when I die.

The sailmaker's face brightened.

—How awful! he said. How wonderful! How awful! And can I say it to myself often?

—As often as you like, said Selah. It's yours now. I thought you would like it. I've been saving it to say to someone of your macabre persuasion.

—Also, said the guess artist, you can mutter

it quietly when someone you don't want to speak to is near.

—That's *true,* said the sailmaker, who had sat down again and begun to stitch once more the massive sail that stretched across the loft floor.

—Until next time, said the guess artist.

1245 —So long, said Selah.

—*À bientôt,* said the sailmaker, with the careful accent of one who has spent time in a French penal colony.

Outside, the street came right up to the sailmaker's loft. It had waited the whole time they were inside speaking to him, and now that they were done, it was ready to go along with them someplace else.

—I was once wrong, you know, more often than two times in three, said the guess artist as they walked.

—What was that like? asked Selah.

1250 They passed by a small shop that sold derelict buttons for trousers and coats and also the right to call yourself a milliner or haberdasher. An old man was sitting in a chair in the shopwindow. At first it seemed that he was dead, but then his nose moved slightly.

—Where does one get that sort of authority? asked the guess artist, examining the man in the window.

—Presumably, said Selah, there is some sort of credential process. Involving perhaps the kissing of a royal hand, and being raised up, etc.

They continued.

—In answer to your question, said the guess artist, it was taxing. People are often offended by wrong guesses as to their thoughts. At the moment, the effect of this is bearable. Often I manage to get only one wrong guess prior to the right one. However, when I had to guess five or six times, the customer would many times stalk off or say cruel things. I never liked that.

—Perhaps we should hire a car, said Selah. 1255
After all, there isn't much time.

Just then a car pulled up, an old roadster from the thirties. A woman who looked very much like Sif was driving it.

—Need a lift? she asked.

—Yeah, said Selah. What a neat car!

The woman smiled at him through her enormous driving goggles.

—I'll sit in the front, said the guess artist. 1260

They got in, and the car zoomed away at an incredible speed.

A moment later it began to rain. It rained very hard, and people began to close their windows. Those caught outside sheltered beneath the eaves of houses or the awnings of shops. The rain clouds made a broad shadow that stood in every direction for quite a ways. Beyond that, the light of the sun could be seen like a curtain. In a nearby square a girl stood, dressed in a short jacket, a long skirt, and espadrilles, with her hair in a braid. She was in the middle of the square when the rain came, and she had not moved, for someone was to meet her there, and he had not come yet, and she worried that if she moved, then perhaps he would not find her, and it was more important to her to be found than it was to be dry.

And so Mora Klein became a very wet and sad girl as the rain continued and no one came for her. The rain continued, and the inhabitants of that square moved around the edges like small furtive animals, attending to their immediate needs. After a while it ceased, but the sky was still dark. An old man made his way out to the middle of the square where Mora stood. He walked on three legs, two of his own and one made of wood. Mora was crying very hard, and her face was perhaps more wet from tears than from the rain shower.

He came up and patted her on the shoulder.

1265 —There, there, he said. I'm sure it's all right.

—But it isn't, she said. It isn't at all. He's not here, and he should be, and I've been waiting for simply hours, and I can't imagine where he could be, and oh, but it's useless.

She started to cry again.

The old man took out an extraordinarily beautiful and elegant handkerchief and gave it to her to dry her tears. It was the sort of handkerchief that one might be content to be judged by if it was all that remained of one after one's death.

Mora didn't especially look at it, but held it in her hands and used it to cover her face a moment.

—He's probably been held up somewhere, said the old man. It happens all the time. One wants to be somewhere, but one has first one thing to attend to and then another. Not to mention the fact that it isn't in the first place easy to get from here to there, even when one knows where here is and where there is. Not presupposing such a knowledge, how can we be surprised when a person fails to get from one location on our broad-domed earth to another? And furthermore, there are opponents, men, women, beasts, objects, streets, buildings, lairs, condescensions, militancies, a hundred ways and means that oppose any kind of successful action, and most especially the sort of special action that would bring a likely young fellow to your side. For he is a likely young fellow, isn't he?

—The likeliest sort, said Mora, sobbing.

—There was a time, said the old man, when I kept an inn in Som. I had a bird there that would sing to me. It sang very quietly, but sometimes it would sing human songs, and it was those songs that I liked best. Here is one now.

The old man began to sing. His voice was very lovely and obviously a part of something that the world had disposed of in its haste, evidence of a grander, kinder past.

Now as I rode out over London Bridge
On a misty morning early
I overheard a fair pretty maid
A cry for the life of her Geordie

Go bridle to me a milk white steed
Bridle me a pony
I'll ride down to London town
And I'll plead for the life of my Geordie

Mora closed her eyes and felt her way in the darkness of her head. It was a song! Such a fine song. She never had been given such a fine song all alone in a square.

For he never stole ox he never stole ass
He never murdered any
He stole sixteen of the King's wild deer
He sold them in Bohenny

Oh I wish I had you in yonder grove
Where times I have been many
With my broadsword and a pistol too
I'd fight you for the life of me Geordie.

The old man sang for a while, and Mora felt in her head the beginning of a long siege. A wilderness had crept up around a walled town, and the darkness of old woods and far-off places began to grow then, even within sight of where men walked together.

By this she meant in her heart that all the useless things one remembers well just before waking and forgets just after were in fact very important and perhaps all that stood now between herself and oblivion.

A small bird, a sparrow, in no wise capable of the song the old man had been singing, flew down and snagged a hair out of Mora's braid with its sharp little beak. She opened her eyes in shock and slapped at it with her hand, but it dodged sideways in the air and flew off before she could manage another blow.

—How fortunate! said the old man. If that had happened to a Roman general, a great victory would have followed.

But even then the bird was flying off over 1295
the rooftops. It flew west across the rooftops to the river, and headed south along the river until it came to a place where not one but two bridges cross. It flew down beneath the first, and landed upon a stoop. A Chinese man was sitting in a plastic chair. It landed on his right knee, dropped the hair into his hand, and flew off.

Just then a car sailed out of the right side of the picture and pulled up before the stoop. Two men leaped out and the car whisked away. One was very well dressed in a fine suit. The other wore the simple attire of the sort of person perhaps who researches sin in the depths of the Vatican but is not a priest at all and goes often flower picking in the country by himself, never speaking to anyone he sees there.

—Hello, he said in Cantonese.

—Hello, returned the municipal inspector.

In the man's head then, the idea of the bird landing on his knee and dropping the hair. This idea only partly in Cantonese and partly in the contusions of the man's thought.

—(This idea said out loud in just that way by the guess artist.)

The man understood immediately. He held up the hair for them to look at. He gave it to the municipal inspector because he liked his suit very much. The municipal inspector understood and took the hair. He did not understand that it was Mora's hair. The Cantonese man snatched the hair back when he saw that the municipal inspector was going to put it into his pocket the way it was. Very neatly and rapidly, he fashioned the hair into a tiny sculpture of a rabbit, knotting and reknotting it. The hair had not seemed to be very long or thick until the man did this. When finished, he handed the little hair-rabbit to the municipal inspector, who held it proudly upon the palm of his hand.

—Not bad, said the guess artist.

The man gestured with his hand that if they

chose, they might enter the building. This they did. It was an ordinary-enough-looking building, a rather downtrodden three-story affair on a dim street, and above, the westward beginnings of the Manhattan Bridge (which lent a darkness to the whole affair).

Inside, there was a filthy sort of passage that led to either a stair or a hall to the building's rear. As the stair only went up, and presumably the larger portion of what they hoped for was down, they took the hall. It was lined with doors whose filthiness equaled that of their surroundings.

On then to the back of the hall. At the back 1305
of the hall there was a large round trapdoor made of malachite.

The two looked at each other in shock.

—How will we ever lift that? said Selah.

The guess artist reached down and tried to lift it at the edge. It didn't budge. Both tried then to lift it at the edges. Still nothing.

Selah drew out the map once more.

—It seems we must go downstairs in order 1310
to go upstairs, he said. In fact, I drew a staircase and pushed so hard with the crayon that the paper is broken. It doesn't say anything about a malachite door.

—What if we both jump on it?

They tried that. It made a loud, hollow sound, but nothing happened other than that the noise of their jumping attracted the Chinese man, who came down the hall. He shook his head at them and said something to them in Cantonese. They did not know what he had said, but they got off the malachite plug and stood dutifully patient by the near wall.

He knelt down and pushed on one section of the malachite. The disc spun up then, revealing a ladder on one side leading down. Selah inclined his head to the Chinese man in thanks, and the guess artist bowed. Then down the ladder they went. It is a curious thing about such ladders. One doesn't know what is at the bottom, but because there is a ladder, one feels comfortable enough to go. Were there simply a craggy cliff face that was perhaps just as easy to climb as a ladder, the whole affair would seem more forbidding. But the fact that a human being has put in place a system for getting up and down in some way pleases, gratifies, and comforts us. Which it shouldn't, as men are the ones most likely to construct difficult and irrational traps, having as their purpose only to confound us.

—What I like best, said the guess artist, is when at Coney Island on the boardwalk the farthest distances of the sea come up very close and quietly to the edge of the sand to surprise me. HELLO, they say, and I greet them with a small shyness of smiling and inclining of my hand. Also, then the slanting of the light in deference to the occasion and the sudden and impulsive gladness of the bathers. Naturally they are insensible to the reason for this business of the waves and myself and the sunlight. However, effect always supersedes rationale, and they themselves, basking in the junction of the various elements, grow large in the world's esteem and are therefore suffused with the pleasure that is at the core of the sweetest and most delectable fruit.

Meanwhile, the municipal inspector was 1315
examining the door that was at the bottom of the ladder. It was a very ordinary door and had no molding or other ornament to help it put its best foot forward. Only a key-sized lock and a small gap where it met the floor. Not even a knob awaited them there.

—As I see it, he said, either we have the key to the door or we put something underneath it, a message of some sort. Or we knock. Or we break it down.

—I don't know, said the guess artist. Perhaps if we wait here someone will come and open it.

Instead, the municipal inspector set his hand upon the door and gave it a little push. It swung gently open, revealing a very fine wood-paneled room. Whereas above there were many different rooms, and the narrow hall down which they had walked, as well as a section including the bottom of the stair, here there was only the ladder's terminus and one broad room beyond the door that took up the entire space.

It was well furnished in a nineteenth-century American style and looked much like the sort of club that a robber baron might have frequented when in search of a cigar, a whiskey, and a good sit.

1320 —Finally, said the guess artist. I've been waiting my whole life to find a place as comfortable as this.

He sat down in one of the chairs and let out a great sigh of pleasure.

Selah sat also. At the far end of the room was another door.

—Do we go there next? he said out loud.

—I wonder why he sent us here, said the guess artist.

1325 —What was he thinking when he said it? asked Selah.

—Nothing much, really, said the guess artist. Something about cornfields and mausoleums.

They sat in silence. On the walls were paintings of the American presidents all the way up to Theodore Roosevelt. The quality of the paintings was very high. Just then they could hear the sound of steps. Then the sound of a key in a lock. The far door opened, and a boy stepped through. His name was Morris. He was concerned with the events that were passing and wanted a part in them very badly. Thus, once before, his father had let him out of the tower in which they lived and which they had sworn never to leave. Now, again, the father had dispatched him on an errand of much importance.

—Hello, he said. My name's Morris. I'm very good at walking far and at climbing trees.

The guess artist and municipal inspector gave the boy encouraging nods. They both felt very strongly that these two occupations as a boy could lead only to a happy and proper future.

—My father said that you should come 1330
down to the bottom. It is a very long way and will take you some time. I brought sandwiches and a thermos of coffee that we can have after a few hours' walk. Then we can walk awhile more, and sleep for the night. If we get up early we should be able to reach the bottom by midday tomorrow.

Disbelief was evident in the faces of the two visitors.

—No, said Morris. It's true, as you will very well see. We had best begin now. This way, please.

Morris the far walker and tree climber crossed the room and reopened the far door. He passed through it. After him, then, the two comrades. On the opposite side was a sort of closet with another ladder. Morris was already at the ladder's bottom. They followed him down. This next story was taken up by the beginnings of a huge circular staircase. Selah went to the edge and looked down. Almost immediately he wished that he hadn't.

—Good Lord, he said. That's far.

The guess artist also looked down. 1335

—How can that be? he asked.

Hundreds and hundreds of feet below there was some sort of landing. It was too far down to distinguish really what lay there.

—I could tell you, said Morris, but my father has been waiting some time for visitors, and I shouldn't ruin his fun.

—How can no one know about this? mused the municipal inspector.

1340 To this Morris said nothing.

He began down the stairs. They were broad and carpeted in the middle. The steps had a fine width and were not too steep or too large for easy walking. The banister on the right was a gorgeous mahogany. It was shaped much like a slide.

The municipal inspector's eye darted to Morris when he saw this.

—Yes, said Morris. You and I are of the same ilk. I have thought often of sliding down, but I have not yet mustered the courage.

The municipal inspector moved slowly to the banister. He looked down. It curved in a great sweeping circle around and around all the way out of sight. The wood was perfectly polished and smooth. He began to lift himself up onto it. Then he thought better and stood again on the stairs.

1345 —It is the same with me, said Morris. But one day . . .

They began their walk down. The steps were easy to manage, and the carpet had a fine degree of springiness. The guess artist noticed that Morris was not wearing any shoes. He sat down on a step and removed his shoes also. He set them side by side on the stair.

—Is this the only way out? he asked Morris.

—This and a pine box, said Morris.

—How old are you anyway? asked Selah.

1350 —Nine, said Morris. And a half.

Selah thought about removing his shoes, but if he did then his pant cuffs would trail slightly on the ground, as the tailor had taken the shoes into account when testing the length that the pant legs should be. He worried over the notion of his cuffs trailing over even such a fine surface as that provided by the richly carpeted stair. Well, he thought then, I could roll them up. He took off his shoes, set them beside the guess artist's, and rolled up his cuffs. He took a few steps down the stairs, then returned to his shoes. Out of his pocket he took a small black notebook. He opened it. On the first page it said, *World's Fair SHORTHAND.*

—What is that? asked the guess artist.

—It's all my ideas for the *World's Fair 7 June 1978.*

The municipal inspector tore out a page from the middle. He wrote a short note on the page and stuck it in his shoe. It said:

These shoes are poisonous. Beware. If you 1355
touch them or wear them, the death you will suffer will make every death you have ever heard of or seen seem easy in comparison.

Morris was very impressed with this note. He said so.

—Thank you, said the municipal inspector. I am often leaving notes. I have had much practice.

On then again down the broad and limitless stair. They walked at first for what seemed like hours, but was really not, and then afterwards for what were hours. All the light was provided by mirrored ducts in the wall. As it became dark outside, the stair too grew dark. However, the carpet was of such soft kindness, and the mahogany wood so pleasing to touch, that they found their way easily downwards through the nigh complete dark.

When they had been walking for six hours they reached the first landing. Both Selah and the guess artist had supposed that it was the bottom. It was in fact only the first landing.

1360 —I had hoped, said Morris, that we could get much farther. Evidently this will take longer than I supposed.

He shared out the sandwiches and also the coffee.

—We can't hope, said Morris, to reach the second landing by nightfall. Do either of you walk in your sleep or move about overly much?

—I do, said the municipal inspector. Always.

—Then we had best stay here tonight, said Morris. If we have to sleep on the stairs, you might fall and roll for some extraordinary distance before striking your head against a wall or wounding yourself against the struts of a balcony.

—Balcony? asked the guess artist. 1365

—Yes, said Morris. There are balconies beneath.

The three lay down on the various couches that sat in attendance on the first landing. The couches were very comfortable, and the travelers were tired from their walk. They decided to have a contest to see who could tell the best story.

THE STORY CONTEST WON BY MORRIS

First, the guess artist told a story about a man-faced fish that lived in a green pond on a large estate during the Napoleonic Wars. Napoleon's army happened to pass through that part of the world, and he used briefly that estate as a command post before one or another of the famous battles in which he refused to take anyone's advice and went his own implacable way.

While out for a walk on the estate, considering the best 1370
way to array his troops along the lines of battle, Napoleon passed by the pond in which the man-faced fish lived. Being a man who was fond of green ponds and of private moments before battle, Napoleon lingered by the pond and stared down into its depths. The man-faced fish saw him and swam up to the surface.

—Good day, said the man-faced fish.

—*Bonsoir,* said Napoleon.

—Below, said the man-faced fish, it is neither day nor night.

When the man-faced fish said this, Napoleon suddenly realized the thing that he had been trying to realize all day. If he sent the cavalry down a certain road, thereafter to cross an embankment, slip through several cavalry-sized shadows, and appear on the right-hand side of the map, a small distraction would be made such that his massive columns would be able once more to smash the other army. In his head then too the memory of an onion he had eaten once as a boy. He had eaten an onion and a hunk of cheese and a piece of bread. The mistral had been blowing and someone had said to him,

1375 —That wind has an ill will. It can push a man from a horse, or tear the roof from off a house.

But at the moment they were not near the lands over which the mistral sang. And the man-faced fish had gone back into the depths of the pond.

—I don't know, said the municipal inspector. I think the man-faced fish probably had secret information that helped the little emperor.

Morris nodded in agreement.

—You should check the facts. You might be wrong.

1380 The guess artist allowed that perhaps it hadn't happened exactly like that. It was then the municipal inspector's turn to tell a story.

—Three men arguing in a tree. One has a hand, another a leg, another an eye. Who believes as I do? Who can say my name?

—What kind of story is that? asked the guess artist.

—It's a riddle, said Selah. See if you can figure it out.

Morris got up from the couch and walked over to Selah. He whispered something into Selah's ear.

1385 —That' s right, said Selah. That's the answer.

He patted Morris on the shoulder.

—From now on, he said, we'll call you Morris the solver-of-riddles.

—I would like that, said Morris the solver-of-riddles.

Then Morris told his story, and it was the best one of all. It was a story about an ambition that sifted through the population of a colony over a period of fifty years until it found the several people in whom it wanted to invest. It was the story of the growth of this ambition and the pain and suffering caused by it, as well as the will behind the ambition itself, and the secret workings of the world of which most men are not aware. Also it included a trip to the moon on horseback, and a secret chamber inside of a ring which would fit on your finger but in which you could also sleep the night safely when surrounded by enemies. Both the guess artist and the municipal inspector proclaimed him the winner, and they all went to sleep.

Selah immediately had a dream. In his dream a girl was standing in a square. It was raining and she was getting soaked by the rain. He knew that it was Mora Klein, although he was so far away he knew he could only have achieved this vantage point by being kidnapped in a balloon and strapped to the outside. Nonetheless, his thought now was not for himself but for the girl, who had begun to cry. The sound of her crying reached him, and he felt a great sadness himself. An old man came out into the square and soon had begun to sing to her a song that was itself very sad. A bird shot down out of the sky and fetched a hair out of Mora's braid. Just then Selah woke. He was holding the hair-knot rabbit in his hand. He felt a sense of well-being. He *would* find her. He knew it. He sat then on the stairs. A sort of viewing lens was positioned above the banister. He looked through it, and saw beneath him on the stair, perhaps twenty feet down, Mora in a belled coat with trousers and heavy boots. Mora, standing there, ever so still!

—Mora! he cried, and leaped for the stairs.

But she was gone.

He ran back to the lens, and saw it then for

what it was, a stereoscope pointed at the stairs with a photograph of the stairs, a photograph of Mora on the stairs. When had she been there? He looked again. Mora was so lovely there, looking up at the camera. Who had taken the picture?

He leaned against the stairs and closed his eyes. The others were still asleep. Soon he was also.

1395 Several hours passed.

Morris woke first and roused the others.

—We'd best begin, he said.

They went on down the stairwell and to another landing. Selah went to the edge of this one and peered down. Again he was greeted by a massive depth and a rising dizziness that sent him reeling.

—How? was all he said.

1400 The guess artist looked also.

—*That* there at the bottom . . . he asked. I presume that is not the bottom but only the second landing?

—And beneath it the third landing, and then the true bottom, said Morris.

—Is there food and drink to be had at the bottom? asked Selah.

—Water may be had now, and at every landing, said Morris. My father should be preparing lunch for us; however, we will be late for that, and he may be cross. He is obsessed with punctuality.

1405 —What does he have to be punctual about? asked Selah.

—Not very much, said Morris. Nevertheless . . .

Morris opened a little closet by the head of the stair. Inside was a water fountain. With a different key, Morris started up the water fountain. Selah and the guess artist drank of it. Then Morris did. Then he locked it. Then they began down.

—Such a wide and never-ending stair, said the guess artist, is in danger of ceasing to be a stair to become instead a metaphor of some kind or even an allegory.

—I shouldn't like that, said Morris.

—Let us not think of it again, said Selah. 1410

At that point they became aware of two things. The first was a series of paintings that had begun upon the left-hand wall. The second was the first balcony that had appeared, extending out from the stair into the nebulous middle space of the stair. Every 150 steps there was another balcony. Each balcony was equipped with couches and comfortable chairs, as well as with a reading table or two, and gas lamps. Nevertheless, the little party was not tempted to stop.

They reached the second landing without incident and had more water there.

Morris began to do a little dance. He was obviously very pleased by his own dance, and he cried out to see if they were admiring it as well.

Onward then they proceeded to the third landing. This third stair was a great deal steeper than the others, and there was no longer any carpet. It was, in fact, so steep that they took to holding tight to the banister and descending backwards. This stair also was the longest of the three. The third landing was really hardly a landing at all but only a brief widening of a single step that accommodated a single leather chair, and then a brutal pinching of the stairs, which spun away down at frightening speed.

1415 The bottom could now be slightly made out. It seemed to be a sort of cleared space with grass of sorts and even trees.

—Is that grass? asked Selah.

—You will see, said Morris quietly.

By this time their feet had begun to hurt quite a lot from the walking. Their legs were sore, and their hearts were heavy when they thought of how they would have to scale the stair to leave.

—How did you ever manage to walk up this and present yourself to us in complete readiness for a return trip down the stair? And furthermore, where do you get the food that you eat at the bottom? Presumably you do not grow coffee or keep pigs.

1420 —Every now and then, said Morris, the Chinese man fetches things for us. He leaves them in the ladder chamber below the malachite plug. His family was sworn into this service many generations ago. The deed for the building passes through their hands. More than that I won't say now, other than that I am good at climbing trees and at walking far, and so it is no wonder that I can climb and descend stairs with no trouble in the least.

To make evidence of this, Morris rapidly descended the stairs at the speed he was best used to.

—I will await you at the bottom, he cried, and bring my father tidings.

In moments he was out of sight.

—What a splendid fellow, said the municipal inspector.

—I like to think, said the guess artist, that if 1425
I had been in his situation, I would have grown to be a boy of such evident talent.

—The same, said Selah.

After an undefined period that might have been one hour or three, the stair broadened into its initial comforting width, and the carpet reappeared. The stairs ceased to turn, and led instead out into a broad meadow that stretched in a magnificent cavern.

The cavern was lit from above by what must have been more mirrored passages reflecting light from the sun accurately, easily, and well, all the way down through the earth, so that just as the sun shone upon the city streets, so too it shone at these subterranean depths.

The meadow was beautiful, the grass nicely shorn. Lovely oaks stood, their broad leaves a bright green.

Beneath one, on a small rise of land, Morris 1430
lay, awaiting them.

—Do the trees hold to the seasons? Selah asked him.

—Always, said Morris.

—How do they get enough water? asked the guess artist.

Morris pointed to a stream that ran out of one side of the cavern wall and crisscrossed the meadow. At one end there was a little waterfall that fell into a pond.

1435 There was a little cottage on a hill in the distance. Smoke rose from its chimney.

Selah and the guess artist followed Morris the far walker through the meadow. Here and there were wildflowers. Bees trailed at the edges, and away in a small underbrush, Selah was certain he saw a fox dart by.

—What a wonderful place! he cried, as much to himself as to the others.

—You must tell my father, said Morris. He will be so pleased; I know it.

As they neared the cottage, they saw that a man was seated upon the front step, smoking a pipe. The cottage was an old-style saltbox house such as were built in the eighteenth century throughout the thirteen colonies.

1440 —It is not a big house, said Morris. But it is right for us.

—Yes, said the guess artist. You seem to have done all right for yourselves.

The man waiting and smoking the pipe wore a pointy sort of knit cap, and had a short red beard. His eyes were very green, and his age could not easily be told.

—Corina, he said. They're here.

A woman came out of the door wearing a large apron and a calico-print dress. She was broad, with a grand beaming smile upon her face. She looked just the sort to provide for them a pleasant and welcoming luncheon and afterwards a fine rest.

—Welcome, she said. 1445

Her husband stood.

—I'm Kleb, he said. We live under the mountain.

—I have heard of the people who live under the mountain, said Selah. I never thought to be so lucky as to meet them.

—You are welcome here, said Corina again.

The guess artist took her hand warmly. 1450
Kleb shook hands with the municipal inspector. Morris looked out from behind his folks at the visitors.

—They are very hungry, he said.

—Come in, come in, said Kleb.

In they went. The saltbox house had a fine little kitchen at the back with a Dutch door. As the day was so pleasant, a table had been set out back of the house with chairs and many fine things to eat. It turned out that there was an entire farm laid behind the house and that the little family grew in fact everything that they needed to eat, and that Morris had been somewhat lying, for the only things the Chinese man brought them were exotic substances like coffee and sugar.

—I suppose, said Kleb, that you'd like to know how all this can be.

1455 He took a bite of a thick ham steak, and chewed it awhile before continuing. On the table was more ham, cooked with honey on a spit over a fire, potatoes, pan-fried doughnuts hot and covered in cinnamon and sugar, leeks, string beans, corn on the cob, and lovely miter-shaped loaves of bread that had just come out of the oven.

—Yes, said Selah, between bites of doughnut. I would very much like to know everything that you have to say. I am looking for a girl. I know that she was on the stairs. I've seen a photograph of her there, and . . .

—We shall save such conversation for evening, said Kleb. It is better suited to the darkness. All tales are, don't you think?

He looked them over in turn.

—You, he said to Selah, you are the municipal inspector. Am I right?

1460 —Yes, said Selah, producing his badge.

—We have no use for that here, said Corina. Put it away.

Selah put it away, more than a little ashamed.

—I'm sorry, he said.

—She doesn't like such talk at table, whispered Morris.

1465 —And you, said Kleb to the guess artist. What do you do?

Corina looked very carefully at the guess artist. So too looked Morris and Kleb. They examined him in a very thorough fashion.

—Stand up, said Corina.

The guess artist stood.

—Turn around, she said.

He turned around.

—What might you be? said Corina to herself.

—I am a guess artist, said the guess artist proudly.

—He's the best one there is, said Selah.

—A guess artist! said Corina. All right, then, guess what I'm thinking.

The guess artist looked at Corina with the care that she had invested in his own examination.

—You were born, said he, in Martins Ferry, Ohio, the daughter of a butcher. He taught you to read in Latin and Greek, and you ran away from home. You came here by accident when you were sheltering from a snowstorm in the foyer of Six Quince Street, and by chance the Chinese man was coming up out of the trapdoor. Of all things in the world you are most proud of the fact that you can name every Roman senator that ever existed by order of age, geographical origin, chronological election, or name.

—Can you really? asked Morris.

—Of course, said Corina. But I don't like to speak of it.

—You have memorized every inch of Plutarch's *Lives,* and you have long imagined that it would be a splendid thing to illustrate the staircase with those splendid books in Greek script stretching the whole way. However, you haven't the proper brushes or ink to do the job and so it has gone undone.

1480 —Well, I never, said Corina. You are something else.

—I could get brushes and ink for you, said Klèb. You should have said something before.

—All right, said Corina. I would like that very much.

—I was thinking, said the municipal inspector, about writing a book in which whenever a character lies, his or her dialogue is in italics. You would think at first that that might simplify things, but I bet in the end, it would only really complicate them.

—Well, said Morris, who was eating a big piece of buttered corn bread. If it was a detective novel, you would see that someone was lying when that person was talking to the police and then you might think that person was the one who did the murder, but really, everyone lies and maybe the murderer goes through the whole book without telling a single lie. He might just be good at avoiding having to lie. But the readers would be misled into thinking he was not the murderer, just because he seems to tell the truth.

1485 —Yes, said the municipal inspector, thus the business of subterfuge.

Three moments later it was evening. The table had been cleared, the visitors had been shown where they would sleep, and then Kleb had taken the municipal inspector out to the field where the horses graze to sit upon a hill and talk. The guess artist remained with Corina, who was in the midst of baking a sort of sausage bread that the two would take with them on the morrow.

Selah sat on the hill's crest. Kleb sat beside him and placed between his own two feet the unlit lantern. The last light came from the mirrored vents, and darkness descended.

—I don't mean to be rude, said Selah. But we are in a bit of a hurry. We're looking for a girl named Mora Klein. I need to get upstairs, but it seemed like going downstairs was the right way. At least, someone told us so.

Kleb thought about that for a minute.

—I don't know exactly what you mean, he 1490
said. But perhaps after I've explained about what I'm set on explaining, it'll have helped?

—I hope so, said Selah.

—It was a long time ago, said Kleb, that a man named Norburn was digging a well on his property. The year was 1863. The Civil War was on. People were angry. Mobs rioted in the streets. But Norburn began to dig a well. Everyone told him that it was idiotic to try to dig a well through the bedrock in Manhattan, and yet he persevered. Norburn dug down seventy-five feet, which was an extraordinary depth for the time. The digging of the well killed him, for he attempted it in summer, and the heat was too much. He never found water. However, his son, also named Norburn, continued the work. At ninety feet, Norburn struck not water, but an empty passage. The rock fell out beneath him, and he was left clinging to the side of the well. Luckily, there was a rope ladder that he had been using in the first place to get in and out. He climbed back up, fetched a longer rope ladder, and descended. But this got him no farther, for the darkness below was immense, and the space into which he had channeled was huge. He made rope ladder after rope ladder and strung them together, but as far down as he went, the hole went still farther. Finally, his making of ladders, and the business of this well (which was concealed now within a small shelter so that the neighbors would not suspect any strange business) attracted the attention of a federal agent, a man by the name of Bascomb Lefferts.

—How did he find out about it? asked Selah.

—That I don't know, said Kleb, but find out about it he did. Lefferts was a man of some learning, and of great acuity. He saw immediately that there was something here that needed the highest degree of caution. He would brook no interference from local authorities, and so, after examining the hole and descending as far as was possible (a herculean task, since it involved first gaining the strength of arm to pull oneself up and down a several-hundred-foot rope ladder), he set out for Washington. Now, as we have said, the war had been going on some time. Washington was an armed fortress, and Lincoln's ear was not easy to get. Yet Lefferts had a certain reputation himself, and one day he was put into Lincoln's company.

—Sir, he said. Might we speak alone? 1495

Lincoln gestured that the many strange and impetuous avatars and incarnations that accompanied him in the form of bespectacled clerks should be off for a moment about some putative business. They left Lincoln and Lefferts in a pronounced globe of quiet.

—Speak, said Lincoln.

Then Lefferts explained to the great man what it was that he had found. He explained that he had dropped enormous rocks down into the hole, and that no sound had ever been returned up out of it. He explained that one could scale down into the hole for hundreds of feet and be no nearer the bottom. He explained also that lamps lit and dropped also disappeared from sight.

Lincoln then set Bascomb Lefferts at the head of a special task force. He commissioned him with the finding of the bottom of the hole, using any means necessary.

—This may be a godsend in pitiful disguise, 1500
he said.

Lefferts never forgot that. He had the phrase engraved on a small metal plaque, and wore the plaque about his wrist as a constant reminder of his mission. Over the next two years he worked day and night, building rope ladders and lowering himself deeper and still deeper into the hole. So long did the rope ladders become that he began to build hammocks that would accompany the rope ladder in order to provide rest for the tired climber. Finally he despaired even of this, and he had a huge cable made, such as was used to bind clipper ships to trading docks. To the end of this he attached the basket from a balloon. He had a massive winch set inside the now formidable enclosure that surrounded Six Quince Street, and down into the hole he had himself lowered, lanterns in tow.

The winch ran out of rope four times, and had to be restrung. Each time the rope was separated, tied off, then strung together with the new rope and lowered. Finally Lefferts reached the bottom, where we now stand.

At that time it was only bare stone, a wide cavern of bare stone, with a stream running through it.

Lefferts cried with joy and laid himself down upon the cavern floor and spoke once more the words that Lincoln had said: *This may be a godsend in pitiful disguise.*

1505 However, the disguise was no longer pitiful.

Lefferts had himself winched back up out of the hole, and he went immediately again to Washington. He sat with Lincoln and told him all that he had found. Said Lincoln:

—I have thought often of your hole, and of what might lie at the bottom. I am best pleased by this that you have found. Here are my plans for what should be done.

Lincoln had set up a special government

branch, sealed from the rest and with only this single purpose in mind: to build a passage down through the hole, and place at the bottom a replica of a meadow and cottage that he had seen once in a dream.

This was the plan that Lincoln had drawn:

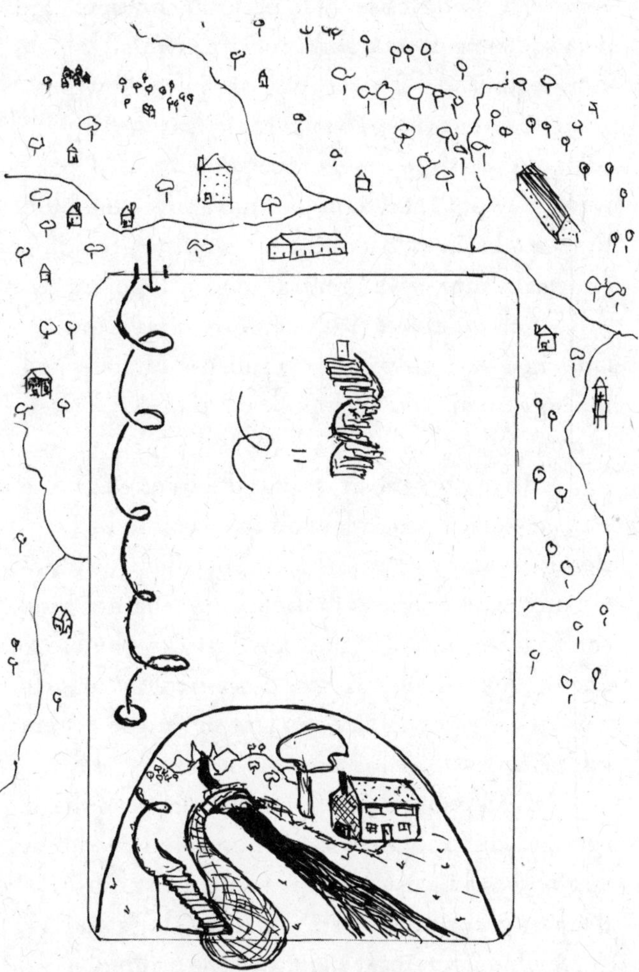

1510 Lefferts returned, now flush with cash, and began the work in earnest. He had to keep the proceedings secret, and so the entire area had to be sealed. A large building was built over the hole, and the work went on underneath, done by workers whose children were kept as hostages in a separate federal camp near the Canadian border.

The building is architecturally unique, because none of its weight relies upon that which is beneath it. All the weight is supported by the stone to either side. The staircase was literally built one step at a time, proceeding down. The workers would stand on the step above, and build the step that would come next, while the building materials hung in the central space supported by the winch far above. Last of all were built the landings, for they prohibited the use of the winch to carry up and down supplies of timber and metal beams.

To import the grass and the trees was no easy task. An ecosystem had to be created where there was none. Perhaps most amazing was the creation of the series of mirrors that enabled the sun to shine upon the meadow just as it shines above. The complication of this mirror system has never been matched by any lens or mirror system built elsewhere at any time in the history of man.

Lefferts himself took up residence in the cottage. He brought his wife down and lived happily to old age. Lincoln passed away during the first year of the work, when the stairs scarcely descended a hundred steps into the ground, and over the next years presidents came and went. No president until Theodore Roosevelt betook himself to see just what the Department of Deep Core Agriculture was accomplishing. When he did, Roosevelt found the existence of the hole. The covering structure had long been removed. A small shack stood on the site, covered around by a stone wall with a locked gate. Within the shack was the malachite plug that you yourself have seen.

Roosevelt descended and spoke with Lefferts, who had gone then into extreme old age. They conversed over the future of the place. Roosevelt decided that eventually, if it were continued to be allowed to manage the place, the federal government would eventually mismanage it. Thus he created an endowment, complete with a board of directors and charter, to see in complete discretion and privacy to the continuation of the hole. He named it Lincoln's Folly, and saw to it that every document pertaining to its existence or creation was destroyed. One more thing he saw to also, and that was to the marrying off of Lefferts's son to a bright-eyed woman named Nancy Rourke. She moved down into Lincoln's Folly, and life continued with no one the wiser.

The Lincoln's Folly Foundation endured 1515
through the Depression. Always they blended the site with the architecture that was around it, so that even down to this day it mirrors the surrounding buildings. The Chinese man who sits outside the door is an employee of the foundation,

and is paid quite well for his services. His own discretion is unimpeachable.

—But, said Selah, all this is really not why I came down here.

Kleb lit the lantern and peered in Selah's face.

—Why ever did you come down here, if not to learn the secret of Lincoln's Folly?

His voice was thick and strange, as is anyone's who has just told such a long and involved tale, only to learn the person listening was not really listening.

1520 —Why, because I want to get upstairs, and I don't know how to get there in the first place, and I was told that perhaps you knew something about it. Or rather, I was told that here I might find out some information that might help me. Whether from you or another, I do not know.

Kleb nodded, and the lantern moved slightly in his hand.

—It's not so easy, he said, to get upstairs. But if you must . . .

—I must, said Selah. There is a girl. She has lost her memory.

—Don't tell me, said Kleb. Listen now. Go into the kitchen of the house. Look at the small painting on the wall beside the spice cabinet.

1525 Selah rose and, taking the lantern from Kleb, descended the hill. The grass felt good upon his feet. A breeze moved, and he could hear in the night the whinnying of the horses. He felt them close by in the darkness, and through it he guided his little light toward the larger light of the house. Soon he came to it. I am so far, he thought, so very far from the world I began in. He thought of Mora, and of his hunt, his long hunt. Around him this small pastoral beauty—to be out-of-doors but indoors. It was a grave and unanswerable pleasure. Somewhere, he felt, there must be a cost paid for a wonder such as this. And also, did Mora come here, and why?

The door was unlocked. He entered. Morris and the guess artist were playing chess. Corina was watching.

—Don't let him cheat, said Selah to Morris.

—When it's his turn, said Morris, I think of all sorts of bad moves that he might do.

—He's very clever, said the guess artist. As I said earlier.

Selah passed through the first room into the kitchen. Corina came after him. Clutching at his hand, she whispered:

—The branch will not break.

Selah looked her carefully in the eyes and saw a few things there that he wished he could remember but knew he never would.

Bread was baking in the oven, and the smell enfolded the house in what seemed like a gentle trembling of longing. Upon the wall beside a cabinet there was indeed a painting. Selah came closer to it. It was very old, a painting of a town as seen from a hill beyond.

—Guess artist, said Selah in a definite you-had-better-come-here voice. Leaned in the corner of the room was a baseball bat. Selah took it up in his hands. Mora, he thought. I will find you soon.

1535 The guess artist came into the room and saw Selah, intent on the painting. He pressed up next to him and peered into the painting.

—Oh, Lord, he said. Here we go.

And the two were standing no longer in a saltbox house at the foot of a great stair, but instead upon a hill in broad daylight. Ahead of them was a signpost. It said:

SOM—>

Selah looked at the guess artist. The guess artist looked at Selah. The road was rather rough, and they were both now barefoot.

—This is a bad business, said Selah. You should never leave your shoes in the midst of a staircase. I knew it was the wrong thing to do.

1540 They started to walk in the direction of the town. The weather was broad, and the clouds were very puffy, while behind, the sky was a deep blue. Ahead upon the road, the town looked fine as well, its roofs and steeples shining in the sun. They made their way down into it, past townspeople laboring in the sun at this task or that, and soon came to an inn.

—This is the inn, said the guess artist.

—Wait here a moment, said Selah.

He burst in through the door. The room was empty. No one was there. Certainly it was the common room of the inn, but the proprietor was elsewhere. All the better, thought Selah.

He proceeded up the stairway that stood on the left. It was a winding stair, but a simple matter for the now experienced stairsman that Selah had become. Up the stair he went and burst into the first chamber at the top.

—Mora! he shouted. 1545

But there was no one there. This room too was empty. In turn Selah went into every room upon the second floor. There was no one anywhere.

Selah returned to the common room.

—Hey, he shouted.

The guess artist came in.

—I don't think there's anyone here, said the 1550
guess artist.

—It's all very wrong, said Selah. I know she's here.

—What's that? asked the guess artist.

The edge of something was sticking out from beneath a table. Selah went around the table. It was a fiddle. He picked it up.

—Let me see that, said the guess artist.

Selah handed him the fiddle. The guess artist 1555
took it and with a violent motion broke it loudly across his knee. The fiddle let out a violent twang.

Out of the broken fiddle there fell a letter, rolled up and tied with a string.

Selah knelt and picked it up.

It said,

WHO WAS THE GIRL IN THE MOTORCAR?

Selah gave the guess artist a puzzled look.

1560 —There are more, said the guess artist.

And indeed, poking out from beneath many of the tables were other fiddles. The guess artist went to the nearest table, picked up a fiddle, and broke it too over his knee. Another letter fell out. He picked it up and showed it to Selah.

UNFORTUNATELY MY FOOLISH LITTLE BIRDS, YOU'VE COME TO THE RIGHT INN AT THE WRONG TIME, OR THE WRONG INN AT THE RIGHT TIME. OR THE RIGHT INN AT THE RIGHT TIME, BUT IN THE WRONG WAY. THAT'S THE TROUBLE.

The guess artist whistled a long, low whistle.

—The wrong way, eh? he said.

1565 Both men looked at each other. Selah's face looked a little strained. He was desperately unhappy, but trying not to show it. The search for Mora Klein had become long and involved, and he wanted very much for her to be found, and soon.

He reached into his pocket and took out the map. He unfolded it.

—What's next? asked the guess artist.

—Let's see, said Selah.

He looked over the map, quietly mumbling to himself.

—Nothing about this, he said.

—Nothing? asked the guess artist. If I had 1570
made a map, then I would certainly have put in something to help us out right now.

—But you didn't, Selah pointed out. I was the one who made the map. And sometimes I wish I hadn't.

He folded it up and put it away. There was a little clock on the wall. It struck nine. Was it nine in the morning or nine in the evening? They couldn't really tell. It was sunny outside of the inn, but that didn't mean anything.

—Let's look at another, said Selah. He grabbed a fiddle and tried to break it over his knee, but he couldn't. For some reason it wouldn't break. He handed it to the guess artist without a word. The guess artist broke it neatly across his knee.

—I used to be in vaudeville, he said with a gentle postvaudevillian smile, and picked up the piece of paper that had fallen.

It said, 1575

TWO MEN descend a stair quite deliberately into the ground. They are guided not by a human being but by a fox that is pretending to be a human being. At the bottom in the den proper they meet a family of foxes. The den is only slightly beneath the ground, under a finely grown oak tree with massive roots. However, the men are persuaded that they have traveled far below the ground. How pleased they are by the den! How happy are their joyous struttings about, how kind their greetings to the fox-man and the fox-wife. A table is set for them, at which they eat not human food, but raw chicken, raw duck, stolen from a farmer's pen. They eat this with relish, are pleased by it, and ask for more. They listen to the stories told by the fox and his wife, and by the dear fox-child for whom they have developed a kind affection. How grand it is that foxes are masters of such secret wishes as this, how grand that they can take men beneath the ground into their dens and guest them as even the greatest kings of Persia could not. Long live the world of foxes and their taking of a thousand shapes. Long live such rascalry, with its quick and supple hand!

—So that's what happened, said Selah. I thought perhaps . . .

—I as well, said the municipal inspector. It wouldn't make sense otherwise.

—Well, they were awfully nice, said Selah.

—Yes, they were, said the municipal inspector, certainly very nice. And the fox-wife, Corina.

Certainly she cooked a fine meal, raw duck or no raw duck.

—Let's read another, said Selah. He looked under a few tables and returned after a moment with two more fiddles.

The guess artist broke the first, and Selah recovered the paper.

THE DOG THAT PLAYS THE FIDDLE WANTED VERY MUCH TO BE A CHARACTER IN THE PAMPHLETEER'S LATEST WORK: WORLD'S FAIR 7 JUNE 1978. BUT IT WAS NOT GOING TO HAPPEN. ALTHOUGH THE DOG CAME TO VISIT THE PAMPHLETEER, AND ALTHOUGH HE REVEALED HIMSELF EVEN IN DREAMS, THE PAMPHLETEER WOULD HAVE NONE OF IT. THEREFORE, THE LITTLE DOG BETOOK HIMSELF TO BE A PART OF THE WF. IN THIS HE WAS SUCCESSFUL. HERE IS HIS SECTION:

---

a Treatise on Fiddle Playing as a Tool for Governance of Happenstance

There are three ways to play the fiddle if one has as his goal the governing of minds. The first way, learned from the rubbing of tree limbs the one upon the other, and from the sitting of rocks quietly on beds of moss, and from the rocking of streams on curving banks, produces notes that lull. In this way, playing thus, one can creep up on a person and render him or her quiescent. THE second way is to climb a lone mountain. First, to find a lone mountain, and then to climb it. Then, to sit upon it and watch the manner in which the various clouds that pass in conversation debate points and make their tiny coups and failures. Their language is the language of distraction. This is the language that the fiddle uses when it wants to rid a person of their own causal thought and make a vacant cloth upon which to paint the letters *it* intends. THE THIRD style of fiddle playing is that of the places that have never seen a drop of rain. These shelters, deep within rock faces, or hollows away beneath the earth, or simply plots of ground shielded always by the thick trees that stand above, have a sort of knowledge based upon ignorance that is always the gravest and greatest knowledge. For the total knowledge, the knowledge of all that may be in the world, is the knowledge of one's death and the world's continuing. That knowledge does not give. It takes away, removing from one peace of mind and fealty of thought. No, the greatest gift is in partiality. And so, from these trees we gain the power to speak lies, to say things that are not true and place them delicately into the minds of those we would conquer.

Selah took this note and put it into his pocket.

1585 —I'm definitely going to put that in my *World's Fair,* he said.

—You should, said the guess artist. I wonder if it's true.

—I myself have no doubts, said Selah.

The guess artist broke the second fiddle. Out of it, this:

THE QUESTION OF MORA

—What an odd drawing, said the guess artist. It makes me think of long Russian afternoons during which no one speaks, not because they are tired, but because they are all very quietly angry at one another.

—It reminds me of that too, said the munici- 1590
pal inspector.

Just then the municipal inspector heard a noise above. He made for the stairs, the guess artist behind him. Up the stairs they flew, and into the first room. No one was there. The municipal inspector looked about. The room was a simple one: a bed, a table, a chair, a lamp, a window. On one wall, a sconce with a candle. Not even a mirror. But, ah, he thought. There is a closet.

The guess artist slipped past him and threw open the door to the closet.

Within, an odd sight greeted their eyes. A half-naked woman, her skirt pulled up to her waist and her blouse pulled down, was rocking in the embrace of a coarse-looking man similarly unclothed. They looked displeased at having been disturbed.

—Who are you? asked Selah. What are you doing here?

1595 The woman and man did not stop what they were doing, or respond. Their noises were both grueling and unkempt. Selah looked away.

—I asked you what you were doing here, said Selah again.

The coarse-looking man whispered something in the ear of the woman. She giggled. He reached out of the closet, still rocking the girl back and forth, and took the door boldly out of the guess artist's hand. Turning to look at Selah, he spat once upon the ground and then slammed shut the closet. Immediately then, a sort of moaning began.

—How awful, said the guess artist.

—Have you ever seen such . . . ? asked Selah.

—Not in a hundred years of Sundays, said 1600
the guess artist.

They checked the other closets on the upper floor, but there wasn't much to be found other than:

LIST of THINGS they FOUND

1. a Colt Navy revolver from 1851, loaded, with holster
2. a child's boomerang
3. a mask from commedia dell'arte
4. a mechanical bird
5. a box with something wriggling inside of it
6. a spyglass

Selah went to the window in the tiny room where the spyglass had been found. In the distance the rolling hills continued. Here and there a homestead or farmhouse might be seen, with perhaps a trail of smoke rising.

He put the spyglass to his eye.

—Mora! he said.

For in the spyglass he saw the inn, and 1605
through a window of the inn he saw Mora standing with a stunningly beautiful woman who could only be Ilsa Marionette, Loren Darius's wife.

—There you are, he said.

He watched her moving about the room, twisting and turning, speaking with her back to him, and going sometimes to the window.

She is looking for me upon the road, thought Selah. Mora! he wanted to cry out, I'm here in the inn. But it was no use. He set the spyglass down a moment and looked out again at the landscape. Then he picked it up and looked through again. This time it only magnified the distant hills. He shook it.

The guess artist was standing in the door watching him.

1610 —I found this, he said, holding up the pistol.

—Give it here, said Selah.

He belted the pistol on. It was rather heavy.

—Do you know how to use one of those things? asked the guess artist.

—Can I hit a target a hundred feet off? asked Selah in reply. No. Can I point it at someone's head and say something desperate, inevitable, and disastrous? Yes. Can I shoot a horse with a broken leg in order to put it out of its misery? No. Can I shoot a man in the leg in order to cause him misery? Yes.

1615 —I thought as much, said the guess artist. Also, there was this.

He put a box onto the table. It was wriggling.

—What do you think is in there? asked the municipal inspector.

—I have an idea or two, said the guess artist. Should we open it?

—We'd better not, said Selah. Anyway, there are more fiddles downstairs.

The two returned to the common room. 1620
They piled up all the fiddles in one place and pulled up chairs. The guess artist broke the first fiddle that was to hand across his knee. A photograph was in it. The guess artist held it up, examined it, and then passed it to Selah. The picture was of Selah, clad in his municipal inspector garb, holding on his arm a very pretty girl.

—That's Sif, said the municipal inspector. She's a girl I know.

On the back of the photograph there was some writing. It said:

If you don't think of me at least once each day, then I will disappear entirely and no one will ever see me again.

Sif

—Do you think it's true? Selah asked the guess artist.

—It's just a threat. Nothing to worry over.

The guess artist broke open the next fiddle. 1625
This note was covered in sheet music.

Selah picked up one of the unbroken fiddles. Many bows were lying about, one for each fiddle. He took one.

—Hold that music up, he said to the guess artist.

The guess artist held up the music.

—Do you play violin? asked the guess artist.

—Sometimes, said Selah. But badly.

Yet somehow this fiddle would not allow poor playing. Selah drew the bow over the strings, and the little melody that was writ upon the note sprang forth with a shimmering beauty. It was a simple little tune, but quite fine. Selah played it several times. On the third time, one of the fiddles at the bottom of the pile burst open. Selah put down the one he was holding, pushed the other fiddles aside, and found the broken one. An envelope was inside. Within that, there was a folded newspaper article, a thick one. It was yellowed around the edges.

He held it up.

—This is the one, he said.

On the envelope it said:

For the Lucky Fool who Comes This Way Unknowingly

The guess artist nodded and took it from him. He began to read out loud:

KLEIN EXHIBIT AT THE METROPOLITAN

Mora Klein was one of the true phenomena of 1635
twentieth-century art. Born in obscurity on the North Face, in Barrow, Alaska, in the 1970s, she made her first mark at the age of four, when it was discovered that she could draw a straight line. As it was the first documented case of a human having the ability to draw a straight line, she gained instant fame. The little girl would be brought by her parents into scientific laboratories and given the most perfect and expensive styli that could

then be found or produced, and she would be given paper of the finest and most perfect grade. Upon this paper she would draw a simple line, stretching from one side to the other. Yet the straightness of the line was astounding! Even with the most powerful microscopes and the most advanced measuring equipment, no deviation could be found in her lines. Even the best machines at that time (and indeed since) deviate. But not Mora Klein.

Scientists thus spent a great deal of time studying her nervous system and the muscles of her arm and hand. But they could not come up with an explanation short of dissecting the little girl on the spot. And many, in fact, in the scientific community were in favor of such a course. If the girl had not received the media attention that she had, it is likely that such a thing would have come to pass.

In any case, Mora continued to grow and draw straight lines. She did not follow her first feat with another for eighteen years. Then, at the age of twenty-two, she made a drawing. It was her first drawing. Prior to that she had only ever drawn lines and done handwriting. It had never occurred to her to do a drawing. She has stated in interviews that she had attempted very carefully in her handwriting to make each writing of her letters change slightly so that it would appear as the handwriting of others, where the shape of letters deviates wildly from occasion to occasion. Yet in her drawing, she brooked no such deviation. She drew the drawing for the first time upon a canvas with a large stylus and a bottle of ink. Instantly it was taken up by the art community.

However, a week later, when Mora drew her second drawing, it was no different from the first. It was, in fact, exactly the same as the first in every way. The drawings were immediately subject to intense scientific analysis. No two things in the world had ever been so precisely alike. They were shortly thereafter bought up by the government for a pittance.

This didn't bother Mora. She continued to produce her drawings. They continued to be precisely the same, and the art community took them up with a glad fanfare. Someone else, a toady of hers, would number the drawings delicately at the bottom to indicate the date upon which they had been done.

Her fame grew. Her drawings sat upon the 1640
walls of the Metropolitan Museum, of the MoMA, of the Art Institute of Chicago, the Tate Modern, the Musée d'Orsay, the National Gallery, the Museo Nacional del Prado, the Smithsonian. Her fortune too was made, for after the sale of just a few she had made enough money to last her the rest of her life.

But Mora was a young woman. She had never really attended college, instead having been tutored privately by professors interested in her peculiar circumstances. This was an arrangement made for her by The New School in New York City. She lived in a flat on the Lower East Side, and finished a B.A. in Political Mythology in two years.

At the time of this article, a retrospective of her work, **MORA KLEIN, the Architect of Similitude,** is being shown at the Metropolitan Museum of Art. Tickets are $12 in addition to the ordinary donation fee. The museum's hours are: Tuesday, Wednesday, Thursday, and Sunday from 9:30 a.m. to 5:30 p.m., Friday and Saturday from 9:30 a.m. to 9 p.m. The Metropolitan Museum is closed on Monday.

—Hmm, said Selah. So that's what she does. No wonder I like her so much.

Wrapped up with the newspaper article there was a reel of 16mm film.

1645 —We have to watch this somehow, said Selah.

—But how? asked the guess artist. There aren't any projectors here.

Selah sat, thinking. The common room was very quiet. All around the floor were pieces of broken fiddles. The guess artist took something out of his pocket and wound it up. He let it go and it fluttered around the room before landing on the table in front of them. It was a mechanical bird.

—Cooo, it said.

—Where did you get that? asked Selah.

1650 —Upstairs, said the guess artist.

—Cooo, said the mechanical bird again.

It flew up around the room once more, banged against the window, flew about, and landed on Selah's shoulder.

—Anger is the artifice of the weak, it muttered into his ear. Only in cold quiet can a man do the true evil that is in his nature.

Selah slapped the bird off his shoulder. It bounced off a wall and was smashed to bits. Immediately the room was full of mechanical birds that flew about, their wings fluttering in the air. They were all muttering, all muttering about the same thing.

1655 The guess artist took shelter beneath a table. But the municipal inspector stood up to better hear what was being said. He could make it out just barely, through their muttering repetitions and interventions.

—A man was building a bridge. It was the longest bridge he himself had ever seen, though perhaps it was not so long a bridge as might have been.

Another said,

—A bridge was in the midst of a man. It was a wild and unknown bridge and it despised everyone who passed across it. The man was a recreant miscreant with a deviant bent who lent himself easily to foul causes.

—Recreant deviant miscreant! called out another bird.

1660 —What's going on up there? asked the guess artist.

—They're telling a story, said Selah.

Just then a bird flying incredibly fast fetched up against Selah's head. He fell over onto the ground and lost consciousness. All the birds landed en masse around him and gathered close by his ears, continuing their muttering. The guess artist was afraid to come out for fear of what might happen, as the house had begun to shift and groan.

—We must be what was inside the wriggling box, he said quietly.

—I think I saw an old cinema a few buildings back, said Selah.

1665 They ran away back down the staircase and out the door into the street. Sure enough, from the spot where a stone was thrown to, another stone might be thrown and strike a theater. The street was still empty. Into the theater. The theater was unlocked. The theater was empty. It was dark, and there were, as far as they could tell, no lights.

Selah found a ladder and clambered up. The guess artist made himself comfortable in some middle row, slightly left of center. The seats were of wood, but finely molded.

Up in the projection room, Selah threaded the film. There was a crank with many gears to turn it at a constant speed. Selah set himself to cranking. But there was no light. Behind him on the wall he saw a plate and a hook. He unhooked the plate and it slid away, revealing an aperture. Through it, tremendously focused light shot straight at the projector, and through the projector onto the far wall. Selah threw himself into the cranking, and upon the screen . . .

. . . an avenue could be seen wandering from left to right. It was full of people, walking as of an afternoon. In the foreground a man and woman were talking. Their voices could be heard easily, with or without sound.

The man was the pamphleteer. The woman was Sif.

—The restaurant is just here, around the 1670
corner, said Sif.

She was wearing an odd sort of dress called a *clavier.* It was very popular during the year 1918. Since then it has seen little use. Nonetheless, it was a fine outfit, and she looked a hell of a knock-out. Especially since she was vexed, and therefore not a little ferocious, and in old movies, being vexed and ferocious always adds a certain degree of attraction to the countenance of a woman.

—I'm sorry I was late, said the pamphleteer. I was one of the riders on the Pony Express and I was waylaid by Indians.

—That is obviously a lie, said Sif. Anyway, if you really had been waylaid by Indians or Native Americans, and taken back to their village and allowed to live there in their midst as one of them, the fact of the matter is that you probably would not have come back. Statistical evidence proves that most of the whites who were brought into the Native American way of life did not want to return to the settlers' villages. Whereas Native

American prisoners in the colonies took every opportunity to escape or even kill themselves.

—Hmm, said the pamphleteer. That's something to consider.

1675 They had reached the restaurant. It said TUNISIAN IMPORTS on the front. They went inside. There were stacks of presumably Tunisian goods of every kind, some in barrels, others in glass bottles, others in short casks. There were no tables or chairs. A man was sitting on a stool behind a counter. He had a cigar box full of cash and an abacus.

—We're here, said Sif. Reservation for Aloud. Sif Aloud. Table for two.

—This way, mademoiselle, said the man.

In the back of the store, through a door behind the counter, was a small room with a single table and two chairs. There were candles lit on the table. The sound of a classical guitar being played somewhat inadequately was coming quietly from somewhere above.

They sat.

1680 —Do you remember the first time we met? asked Sif.

—I'm not sure, said the pamphleteer. Was it on the docks when the city was being evacuated?

—No, said Sif. That must have been some other girl.

—I'm sure it was you, said the pamphleteer. You weren't wearing any underthings, and we went into the shadow of the trees and . . .

Sif blushed and gave him an angry look.

—That was definitely some other girl! How 1685
awful.

—Oh, said the pamphleteer. I thought that was you.

—No, said Sif. We met at that party, the one given by that photographer who leaves cadavers in public places and photographs the neighborhood on time lapse to see how the patterns of movement change.

—Cors Vanderwall, said the pamphleteer. That sick bastard.

—Yes, him. I had met him while hang gliding on Maui. He has a house there.

—I'm sure he does, said the pamphleteer 1690
crossly. He's had no end of good luck.

—Anyway, you had met him somewhere, and so we were both at the party. I was out on the terrace smoking a cigarette. Someone inside had started a discussion about the death penalty. Apparently Cors had managed to get the body of a fellow who had been killed by lethal injection in Texas, and he was intending to put the body on the ground either in Times Square or in Astor Place. He hadn't decided which would be better. The whole thing made me feel sick to my stomach, so I went out to the terrace. You were sitting there, writing in your notebook.

—*The World's Fair Shorthand,* said the pamphleteer proudly. I had just begun it. *As a child, they could not keep me from wells.*

—*As a child, they could not keep me from wells*, eh? said Sif. I read that one too. It's the last one in that little Irish book.

—But which book, and which Irishman? asked the pamphleteer.

1695 Sif shook her head.

—It doesn't matter. The words are more important than their author. Anyway, it was then that I asked you to read me what you had been writing, and you told me the most peculiar story about a goat.

—Oh, my God, said the pamphleteer. I totally forgot about the goat.

—Do you mean to say, asked Sif, that you didn't put the goat in?

—Not yet, said the pamphleteer. But there's still time. That was the goat that could do puzzles, right?

1700 —Yes, said Sif. I believe it could also crochet.

A woman came into the room. She was very tall and wearing a long leather apron. At her side was a large cleaver, hanging from a loop on the apron.

—Hello, she said. You pay first. One hundred dollars each.

—A hundred dollars? said the pamphleteer to Sif. Really?

—Yes, she said. This is a nice place.

1705 Sif untied a scarf that was wrapped tightly about the smooth upper reaches of her arm and took two hundred dollars out.

—You can pay next time, she said.

The woman accepted the two hundred dollars and tucked it behind her ear. She unhooked the cleaver, raised it up in the air, made a loud shouting noise, and slammed it down into the center of the table.

The pamphleteer and Sif leaped back in their chairs. The cleaver had sunk at least two inches into the tabletop. Now they noticed that upon the tabletop there were many such marks.

—The meal begins, said the woman in a quiet voice that had only ever been used just after slamming cleavers into wooden tables.

She left the room and returned a moment 1710
later with a beautiful bottle of wine.

—Chez Margot, she said, and poured them each a glass.

The pamphleteer tasted it.

—Lovely, he said. Just lovely.

The woman disappeared again and returned, this time with figs that had been stuffed with goat cheese and baked while wrapped in thin strips of moist lamb.

—Not bad, said Sif. 1715

She took a bite and leaned back in her chair with a happy, distracted look on her face.

—Did you hear the latest bit of that business with Mora Klein? she asked the pamphleteer.

—No, he said. Who's Mora Klein?

—The artist, Sif said. You know, she does that drawing, like this.

1720 —I think I've seen that before, said the pamphleteer.

—Yes, well, anyway, said Sif. It turns out that children who are shown this drawing at an early age, and forced to look at it for long periods of time, say by having it on the walls of a nursery, have had their brains develop differently in such a way that they are able, at the age of five or six, to do complicated math and logic problems in their heads. The only strange thing is that they can't explain how they know the answers; they just know them. Somehow the relationships between numbers make more sense to these children than they do even to the best mathematicians. Scientists who have studied the drawing say that it has to do with the precise angles involved. Facsimiles and copies of Mora's drawing are not similar enough to the originals to achieve this effect. Only the originals accomplish it. Thus parents have begun to bring their children every day to the Metropolitan Museum to stare at the drawings for a while. The place has been mobbed. There's been talk of creating a special viewing room. The price of her drawings has shot through the roof. They were already expensive. Now they simply can't be bought unless you have more money than a bank.

—Good Lord, said the pamphleteer. What does she have to say about it?

—She won't talk to the press. She lives now somewhere downtown in New York City and tries to have an ordinary life, but it's difficult. Apparently international aid organizations are contacting her, trying to get her to start producing her drawings again, this time for charity.

—So, said the pamphleteer, the kids who were looking at these drawings while they were growing up can just take numbers and combine them in crazy ways?

—Yes, said Sif. Although, it doesn't seem 1725
like it will be useful to our mathematics. The kids don't seem very interested in math. They all think it's too easy. None of them want to go into it because they don't understand the way we do math in the first place. They started in a different way, and the ways can't be combined.

The woman arrived again in the room, this time with a clay case in which had been baked an entire lamb.

—This is koucha, said Sif, getting her fork and knife ready.

The woman returned a moment later with couscous, a little cake, something that looked like ratatouille, and a soup.

—That's chakchouka, bouza, brik, and chorba, said Sif, who was obviously very pleased with herself.

The woman, who now lingered at the room's edge, also seemed pleased at Sif's knowledge of Tunisian cuisine.

—Anyway, said Sif, we were talking on the balcony, the first time we met, and then we left together and went to a different party, the one on the rented subway car.

—That one, said the pamphleteer. That one I do remember. We rode on the roof when it went over the Williamsburg Bridge.

—Yeah, that was fun, said Sif. But we got awfully dirty. They don't clean the roofs really enough, at least not enough to make it a clean business to ride on top of the subway cars. Anyway, I told you that I wanted to show you my place. We got off somewhere and took a taxi. After a while we got back to my place. We had just gotten through the door, and then you said to me:

—Let's pretend that we've never met before. I just invented a criminal organization that can have two members. I think you should join it. I'll go back outside, knock twice, then four times, then once. That'll be the signal for you to whistle. You whistle once. Then I'll knock once. Then you let me in. I'll come in, and pretend that we have never kissed before. I'll touch your face with my hand and run my finger along your cheek. Then you kiss me. Then we talk about what crime we are going to pull off.

—All right, said the then-Sif. 1735

And so you went back out the door. I shut it after you and waited. After about five minutes you knocked twice. I waited. You knocked four times. I waited. You knocked once. I tried to whistle, but I couldn't. I just couldn't; I don't know why. So I ran to the stove and I put just a small amount of water on to boil. I'm sure you were waiting in the hall, wondering what was going on. Anyway, finally, the water began to boil. I was jumping out of my skin waiting for it. It let out this shrill, shrill whistle. You knocked once more, and I threw open the door.

Then you came in, looking at me in this funny, I-have-never-seen-you-before sort of way. I smiled. You reached out and touched my face, and then I came closer to you. I came closer and then closer still and started to kiss you. Your hands moved around me, and I felt bathed in the odd sort of light that I had always hoped would accompany my life. Afterwards we lay out on the roof on blankets and talked of what crimes we would commit.

—I think, said the pamphleteer, that you're thinking of a different guy. I'm not that clever.

—I know who I'm thinking of, said Sif, taking a sip of her wine.

1740 A little turtle had come into the room. It rubbed up against the pamphleteer's leg. Somehow there was no longer anything on the table. It had happened, as it sometimes does in good restaurants, that the waiter was able to remove everything from the table without anyone noticing. The pamphleteer lifted the turtle up onto the table. There was a note tied to its leg. He took the note and opened it. The note said,

---

Without pause then, the municipal inspector returned to the Seventh Ministry. The streets were loud with winter, that is, loud with the winter sort of quiet that the snow brings. Amidst it, the municipal inspector hurried. He wore over his customary gray-blue suit an overcoat as well as gloves and the sort of hat that a fighter pilot would wear when not in his plane.

He crossed the small park that adjoined the Seventh Ministry. No one had shoveled the walkway.

He said to himself then, Either no one is there, which has never happened, or all this snow has fallen since they arrived. Or, he added, they arrived by a different route.

He opened the door and entered. Rita was sitting behind her desk wearing a strapless thin wool dress with a pair of wool mittens tied together and thrown over her shoulder, one in front, one behind. Her hair was up in a French braid, and she was in the midst of writing out a message.

—You! she said. You were supposed to 1745
meet me yesterday for tea at the Covenant Café in the old subway station. What happened?

—I'm sorry, said Selah. I was imprisoned in a Victorian house by a cruel man named Patrick and his crueler wife, a woman named Caroline.

—I don't believe that at all, said Rita the message-girl. If so, how did you get out?

—I don't remember, said Selah. The circumstances are unclear.

—Ah, said Rita. What if I were to say, The circumstances are unclear; I don't know what happened to your messages? What if I was to say, the circumstances are unclear, I don't know what happened to the person who is upstairs waiting in your office? He has been here so long that I had to bring him four cups of tea and four petit fours.

—You're a darling, said Selah. I will make it 1750
up to you. You remember that Darger original I stole from that Wall Street office? I'll give it to you. It has the little girls all rolled up in carpets.

Rita's eyes flashed with sudden delighted avarice.

—Really? You will?

—It's yours, said Selah.

After all, he thought to himself, I have three others, and it's not fair for one person to have that much of a good thing. Not fair at all. I wonder what would happen, he thought, if a child stared at Darger artwork the entire time he was growing up. Would he be able to do a strange mathematics that no one had ever conceived? Or would he just become very good at helping little girls who were engaged in child-slave rebellions?

1755 —Upstairs, you say? asked Selah.

—Yes, he's upstairs, she continued.

Selah hurried down the hall, climbed up the ladder, and passed through his own fine door into his glorious, comfortable, lovely office, a place he delighted in and was always happy to return to. Seated upon a leather sofa in the center of the room and staring calmly out the window at the falling snow sat Selah's uncle. He was holding in his hand a copy of a book. On the cover it said:

WF 7 J 1978

—Have you read it? cried out Selah suddenly.

—I have, my young man, said his uncle, standing and giving to Selah a resounding hug, the sort of hug that can be given only in winter when one is wearing a great quantity of clothing.

1760 —And? asked Selah. Did you like it?

—My boy, said Selah's uncle, it is a very

fine piece of work, very fine indeed. Nothing like those first stumbling attempts that I heard tell of at the start of your career.

His uncle flipped through the WORLD'S FAIR. It was filled with diagrams, typographical displays of excellence, painted pages, watercolor glimpses of pyramids from 1912, photographs of French villages in the fifteenth century, names of obscure people who had figured prominently in history without any credit. He flipped through its pages slowly and delicately. Selah could tell by the way that his uncle touched the pamphlet that he had for it a large and careful affection. Selah's heart swelled.

—I think, said his uncle, that it was the right thing, the very right and proper thing, to install you here. This Rita is a swell gal. Levkin of course is Levkin, and not to be spoken about save in great need. However, we will note in passing his great importance to the life of the city. And the Seventh Ministry itself, why, I had not been down here in some time. You have made quite a comfortable place for yourselves here.

Just then the intercom on Selah's desk started to shake. Selah pressed a button.

—Selah, it's Levkin. We've got something 1765
else for you to see.

—All right, Mars, said Selah. I'll be down in a jiffy.

He released the button and turned back to the room.

—Make that two jiffies, said his uncle. I have one more thing to tell you.

Selah pressed down the intercom again.

1770 —Make that two shakes of a cat's tail, he said. Rather than a jiffy.

—Noted, said Levkin. Over and out.

Selah's uncle had gone over to the window. He pressed his hands up against the cold glass. He could feel the cold of the streets now on his fingers, the cold of this city that was his, he felt, more than any man's. For it was to some degree this man's power that infused the city and ran it from day to day, although he was no mayor, and he went unnamed each day down the avenues. In his head he thought, When I was a young boy, out in the lots and playgrounds of my small town, I never dreamed that there would be so many worlds between that day and this.

Selah took his coat off, hung his hat on a hook, folded his suit coat and settled it over the back of a chair, rolled up first his left sleeve, then his right, leaving his left sleeve less rolled, and joined his uncle by the window.

—What more? he asked.

1775 —A dog would lie and tell you that it has not been petted yet on a given day no matter how many times you were to pet it. This is the way with dogs. They want to be petted, to be joined by their master and let live in his radius. What is a lie to a dog? They do not place things in human places. To a dog, whatever brings his master close by is good, and whatever keeps him away is bad. This is how all morals work.

—I believe as you, said Selah, though I did not know it was your way.

—Or let us say that a bird decides one day that it can be a man. Well, already it is walking upon two legs. Is it so far for the bird to learn to speak as a man does, to learn to wear clothing, to handle its wings as a man handles his arms, to learn to grasp objects in hands, to come of one's own accord in and out of human spheres, counting oneself a human being?

—It is far, said Selah. How far I do not know.

—Not far, said his uncle. If only you knew the things I know.

He rested his great head against the wood 1780
of the molding. He now seemed not like to Selah's uncle, or indeed to any uncle, but more like to Aslan, the fabled lion of Narnia. Selah longed to be cast through the air by his soft breath, to be told the certain wonders of a bewondered world by this impeccable, imponderable beast.

—There are three ways, Selah. Three ways that you can go if you want to find the vanished Mora Klein. You must go by the inn. That is the same, no matter which way you choose. The first way is to go and speak with Levkin. He is the start of the first path. You will gain Mora more easily, but you will lose someone else forever.

Selah looked at him wordlessly.

—The second way is to come with me. I will

take you somewhere where there may be a way forward. But that way is uncertain, and may not even exist.

—And the third way? asked Selah.

1785 —The third way?

His uncle looked at him with a puzzled expression.

—You just said there were three ways. I heard you.

—I never said that. There are only two ways. But if you thought you heard of a third way . . .

His uncle's face looked like the seventh whisker of a devil-cat intent upon the stalking of its prey.

1790 —If you heard of a third way, then perhaps you should take it.

—But that's the thing, said Selah. I don't know the third way. I only heard of it from you.

—Well, I must be going, said Selah's uncle, who still resembled very much an enormous lion. Are you coming?

—I don't think so, said Selah.

He pulled out his desk chair and sat down in it. His uncle left the room more quietly than Selah would have thought was possible, and Selah was one who took pride in moving quietly.

1795 Selah looked first at one of his hands and then at the other. Hands, he thought. Ordinary hands. What can I do with them? How can I find Mora Klein? He looked up at the wall. Posted there was a drawing.

How well he had forecast his own fate. Selah rose and went into the bathroom. The clocks! He had forgotten entirely about the clocks. Selah rushed back into the room and buzzed down to Rita.

—Yes, she said.

—Rita, could you come up here for a moment?

—One minute, she said.

Selah counted out the minute slowly. On 1800
the sixtieth second, the door swung open and Rita
waltzed in.

—Rita, said Selah. I don't think the clocks *are* three hours ahead. Why did you tell me they were?

—Because, said Rita, I like to perplex you. Everyone does. You're good at not being perplexed, and so everyone wants to ruin your unperplexability.

—Ah, said Selah. Thank you.

Rita spun around. Her wool dress stopped well above the knee, and she wore knee-high socks.

—Rita . . . said Selah. 1805

She looked back over her shoulder at him.

—Yes?

—Would you whisper something in my ear?

—All right, she said, licking her lips like a cat. Close your eyes.

Selah closed his eyes and sat very still. He was wearing a vest, trousers, black shoes, spats, and a white shirt with the sleeves rolled. He rested his elbows on the desk and let his head sink into his hands. His breathing slowed. In his head he thought of the dog he had always wanted, a Kerry blue terrier. They were poacher's dogs, from Ireland, and were not afraid of anything. If only he had his Kerry blue with him, things would be easier. This is how he felt often. Mora, Mora, Mora, he thought to himself, and the snowflakes spun down through the air. In what world were you lost, and which thread have you left me?

—I can do a cartwheel, whispered Rita, and so can you. There were nine outside of the black house, and seven within. Nine defeat seven, but not beyond the walls, and so they waited within while planes passed overhead, and the battle of Britain continued, day after day, in an asylum just north of the Canadian border. Yes, I drove a truck while the war effort made its way south then east along the old road that's now been paved over. I began with the gold rush and told my secrets in a million wild ways in the watery concourses that figure well in man's esteem. I saved every penny I ever made and invested it all in U.S. Steel, and when the war came, my bank burst with gold, and

I bought an island and manufactured servants from the earth like golems, and set them to serve me forever. But I won't live forever.

Selah breathed deeply. Rita's lips brushed his ear.

—I told men the way in which they might improve the world. Instead they improved themselves at the world's expense. I wrote in a ledger the cost of each action, and how all things are linked, and any movement is a crime. I went on holiday as a child with a child, and as children we sat in low boats on the skin of streams and ate from baskets and called out to taller ones and were called out to in our turn. We laughed when we were told that we would one day lose our skin and become piles of bones that had no laughter in them. And we knew too that this was a lie, for once a thing has happened once, it cannot be stopped from happening again and again. Events are continuous, not broken, and they never move on. Stories tell themselves one to another, over and over, never ceasing, and we skip here and there, saying this is consciousness, this acrobatic feat, but what of remaining? What of the story of a stone in a field that is a stone and stays upon an evening when there will be rain but there is not yet, and the last moment of redness is paused about the tiny cloud that lingers on the sketched sky? Yes, the little cloud whose name is Sillen, who himself has seen all the wicked deeds that men to the west have done, and who goes now into the east, with word of new rebellion.

Rita drew a breath, and he felt her body through her thin dress.

—I cannot be sure how long I waited between worlds for this new post. I was a wisp, a saint, a gladiolus, a gladius in the beckoning hand of a gladiator. Who poured water in a windowsill down into the potted plant, longing that I might grow? And the sound from the street below, the courtship of earth and sky, the noise of radios and singing, of revelry. Names bear names upon themselves. They are of no use until afterwards, and at that time they have gone. Three things are required of you: the wishes you made when you first knew the breadth of this life; the contract you signed when you decided your wishes were not true or possible; and the exacting of the punishment you agreed to when you knew you would break the contract of your life.

Rita's lips touched Selah's ear again. He could feel her breath. In her thin wool dress she was trembling.

—There is in the little meadow beyond the mind's reach a steeplechase being run by horses who were once riders of horses. They chase one another, and allow one another to pass in a dancing, laughing way. They cross the paths that cannot be crossed, and they tell the time as it has never been told. Beyond a bank of trees there is a little door, round and made of wood. Someone is behind it, knocking. He has been knocking for hours. Another passes that way. This person, broad-brimmed hat upon cloaked form, stops and unbolts the door. Out of the door steps S., the pamphleteer, the municipal inspector. He looks around at the wide, stretching lawn of the world, everywhere bedecked with huge oaks and stretching canopies that give shade when shade is needed. He is carrying a little bag full of books that he has made.

—Thank you, says S. to the man in the broad-brimmed hat.

—It was no trouble, says the man from beneath his hat. I had supposed that a person would come out from that door one day, and years without end I have walked only upon this road home so that every day there would be a chance that someone waiting to be let out might be let out by me. There are not many who walk upon this road. I have thought often of how it would be. Always in my idea of this moment, the door opened. Out stepped a man in a gray-blue suit, serious-looking but young, carrying a small slung bag.

—Thank you, said the young man in the gray-blue suit each time he emerged.

—It was no trouble, I replied. Will you come beneath my roof for a fine supper? My children are waiting, and my wife as well, away at the edge of the wood.

—I would like that, said the young man in the gray-blue suit.

We walked then along the path where always and every day I have walked come evening and came then soon to my house, which is truly not a house so much as a den, and came then to my wife and children who are my wife and children but who are also foxes, and who are pleased in themselves to be sometimes people and sometimes foxes, or always fox-people, creating illusion with the sweep of a sly grin.

At the door to my den, the young man said,

1825 —But if I go within, is it certain that I will ever come out?

—Not certain, no, I said. What is certain is that you will go in. I can see it in the tilt of your elbows.

For the young man's elbows were tilted in an odd sort of way. From looking at them it was obvious the young man was going to enter the den. Enter he did, ducking his head and stepping inside.

The inside of the den was cozy as could be. A little window was set in the side of a hill, and it shone down through onto a little kitchen. A wooden table was pressed up against the wall with chairs. It was heaped with every comforting sort of food that the young man had ever imagined, scones and pancakes and Danish, doughnuts and waffles and cookies, a turkey, a ham, a London broil, baked breads of every description, butters and cheeses and sausages.

—Sit, please, said the man.

1830 Then out from an inner room rushed the children, and after them the wife, a slender woman with a soft fur that bristled ever so slightly in the wind. Her husband took off his hat, and his muzzle was a proud and handsome muzzle. The children sat about the young man with the gray-blue suit and they asked him for things, and everything that he was asked for he had somehow to give them. One asked him for a pocketknife, and he gave the little fox a pocketknife. Another asked him for a disguise box, and the young man took from his coat a disguise box, ready-made in Switzerland in 1932, of the very best quality, number seven of twenty-six ever made. The third fox-boy asked him for a kite, and from a secret pocket the young man with the gray-blue suit drew forth a fighting kite made in Japan, a kite that would allow the young fox upon a trip to some distant fox-meadow, where foxes kite and play in the windy autumn, to cut the strings of others foxes' kites, and watch them plummet to earth, all the while laughing in that peculiar fox way and dancing about on one's hind legs.

As well, the young man had brought a gift for the fox-wife, a great pottery bowl blessed within it with the image of a morning town.

The town was beautiful, and no one could say its name until the fox himself roused himself from a sudden sort of slumber and said,

—That is Som, where sometimes I have been.

The young man said then that he would rather go there than anywhere, and the fox leaped upon him with his rows of teeth and sharpness and great fox-suddenness and strength and tore open his throat. Then into the bowl the young man's life poured, and it filled the bowl all the way to the brim, and there was in the town of Som a great eruption, and a statue in the westward-tending square facing the west road burst open, the old statue of Marionette. Out of it stepped the municipal inspector.

1835 He leaped down to the ground and surveyed the square. People had come out of stores and houses and were staring at him strangely. He felt at his throat. The skin was unbroken. He brushed the stone dust off the arms and legs of his clothing, and crossed the square towards the little alley that led along the backs of houses to another thoroughfare that in time would reach the road upon which sat the inn. And so in time, a minute or two of walking followed by a moment, and that moment followed by a long moment of thought concerning the depth of a well he had seen once in passing from a horse, and how wells seem different from horseback than they do from afoot, and how they seem different to grown men than to children, and how perhaps the feelings of men and children for wells might not prove a good index for how life has changed a man in general, the better to judge how he might return once again to his grander beginnings. And then he was before the inn.

He approached the door. It was a dark wood, and said something on it in a language that no one living now spoke. He opened the door and entered. To his right there was a bat, leaning against the door. The common room was full of voices. A bearded man came around the bar.

—Hello, he said. You are not early, but you are not so late, either.

The man had a funny look in his eye.

—I am going upstairs, said Selah.

—I expect you are, said the man. 1840

In the background, Selah could see a dog standing upon its hind legs playing upon a fiddle a song he remembered. Another man sat in the corner facing the corner with a sadness of corners and places of ending that Selah could not look long upon. About this man too there was the filthy rag of squandered luck. Selah turned from him then and sprang up the stairs. Yes, up the stairs and onto the landing. This place was as familiar to him now as the house in which he had been born, a little clapboard farmhouse on the edges of a great lake, where questions were often asked, but rarely answered, in training for a larger world.

Selah burst through the door he had so long been standing somehow impossibly before.

In the room, a beautiful woman was sitting upon a rocking chair. She was sewing something, and her needle never ceased its movements, back and forth, darting implacably through the pierced and repierced cloth.

—You are Selah, she said. I am Ilsa Marionette. I did not think you would come through the statue of my father.

—I'm sorry, said Selah. I did not know it 1845
was his statue.

—There are many, she said. It is a good use for a statue, and one to which no statue has ever been put. I think he would be glad to have been a part of it. Grace in circumstance, he always said, was the true matter of life.

—Where is Mora? asked Selah.

For the girl was nowhere in the room.

—She has gone, said Ilsa. She waited quite a while, you know.

Ilsa narrowed her eyes.

—Quite a while.

—I came as soon as I could, said Selah. No one else could have come sooner or swifter. Where has she gone?

Ilsa Marionette smiled, and her smile was the delight of a thousand children placed all in a row in a happy and enduring place.

—Selah Morse, she said. Was Mora ever here? Did she ever come to fetch me away from my husband? Are you not tired from speaking so long? Sleep beckons from every cabinet, from every bed, from every scrap of cloth. Sleep beckons from trunks, from windows, from tree limbs and pie safes. Beneath doors sleep beckons. You are tired, yes. You have spoken so long now. Mora was here, she was here, but she has gone. For an instant she faltered in her thought, and disappeared.

There is a chance, however.

Her voice had changed slightly. She had remembered something hopeful.

—There was a little rabbit made of knotted hair . . . do you still have it?

Selah desperately checked his pockets and then all of his secret pockets. The rabbit was nowhere to be found.

—No, he said. No! It seems to be missing.

—Then there is no hope, said Ilsa Mari- 1860
onette. I don't know what to tell you. I wish it were otherwise. You will never find her. Instead you will continue day and night through nineteen versions of confusion, becoming each day less than you were the day before. Eventually there will be nothing left of Selah Morse. Not even the ink of your calling card.

Selah stood then, looking into the perfect symmetry of Ilsa Marionette. There was nothing there, no clue to any possible solution.

—What of your husband? said Selah. He's downstairs even now.

Ilsa held a piece of embroidery in her hands. It was a dog chasing a dog who was chasing the first dog unsuccessfully.

—If we can both forgive each other, there is a chance we might begin again, she said.

Just then the guess artist entered the room. 1865

—My friend, said Selah, his voice choked. Mora's gone away.

The guess artist put his arm around Selah.

—Is she really gone? he asked.

—Ilsa says that—

—Aren't you tired? interrupted Ilsa. 1870
Haven't you been speaking for a very long time?

Then the guess artist interrupted, making a

loud, galloping, grinning noise. There was suddenly out of nowhere a broad and manifest delight in the depths of his face.

—What is it? asked Selah. Tell me, my comrade, tell me, my brother in arms, you who accompanied me through the snows of the Russian winter, tell me what you see.

It was difficult then for the world to bear the disparity between Selah's grief and the guess artist's happiness, so close together and impossibly cleaved they were. The room shuddered a little, and a lamp went out. Ilsa unshuttered the window and was profiled against it.

—They were a long time in the room at the top of the stairs, said the guess artist. She had been struck by a car that had come from nowhere and gone away afterwards to nowhere. She had been taken to a hospital by a young man whom she had never met. There she had been taken care of well, and it had been found that her memory was lost, perhaps for good, and she had left that place in the company of the young man who had found her. Together they had gone back to the young man's rooms, where his printing press and lithograph machine and the tools of his trade were arrayed all about the spaces and belongings that made up his life. Amidst all this, he gave the girl a cool drink, and then began to speak to her in a layered, tortuous fashion, keeping always her past, and the things that might have been, foremost in his mind. He arrayed before her all the objects of his hope, all the things he wished had been and were, and so then they became what was real, and not imagined, and he placed his life in the context of hers, and together they drifted, questing, through the half-light, his resourcefulness all that stood between themselves and the devil, sleep. And when morning came and the sun arose in the east, the young man was speaking still, and the girl was still and slowly, beautifully, upon his arm, eyes wide, listening carefully to each syllable, carefully to each phrase and word and worded phrase. The whole was sewn together with paragraphs and dashes and went in a whirl around a pamphlet that the young man had made in truth, a pamphlet named WORLD'S FAIR 7 JUNE 1978. And the young man saw that the sun had risen, and the girl saw it too, and there was in their hearts a lightness and a pleasure with the things of this world, and they rose up from where they had been sitting and went down to the street and out into the morning city.

—Selah, said the girl Mora Klein, where 1875
shall we go?

—To the boardwalk, said Selah. It is proper there in morning, with the edges of things curled up. One can look underneath.

—I imagine, now, said Mora, that a taxi will draw up to the curb and we will get into it and the windows will be wide-open and we will drive brilliantly through the streets all the way to Coney Island in a swirling and impetuous fashion, and though things will rise up to stop us, nothing will have any power over a passage as splendid and daring as ours.

A taxi drew up then to the curb, and Mora and Selah got in. They hung from the wide-open windows as it drove at blinding speed through the streets and across a bridge and swept down Atlantic Avenue, down through Brooklyn to that always faraway and close Coney Island.

Then they alighted upon another curb and paid the cabbie with a gold doubloon, and ran up to the timbered boardwalk and the morning sand and mist upon the water.

—Selah, said Mora cautiously, her voice trembling. What about Sif? Is she real? Is she the girl you love? Or is she a version of myself that you invented for me, like the carefullest, most special set of clothes that anyone ever made?

—Sif, said Selah, is the girl I invented in order to fall in love with. I wrote a pamphlet about her in the hopes that she might be. You are the girl who was struck by a car, sent up through the air to land upon her head. You have yet to become what you will become.

—Then I may be Sif Aloud, and I may be Mora Klein, and I may be whom I like, said Mora. I may even be Rita the message-girl, though she gets the worst of it sometimes, always stuck in the ministry offices, never allowed to leave.

—Rita gets to leave, said Selah. Whenever she wants to. If you want, I can introduce you. She's awfully nice.

Mora pulled Selah down to her and kissed him full on the mouth, and he was surprised with the ferocity of the gesture. He ran his hand along her back, and delight coursed along his arm.

—Let us make a pact, she said. To madness 1885
at every juncture!

—To madness! said Selah.

They were very close together, and this was immensely pleasing to the both of them. She pushed her face and cheek against his very hard, and he pushed back. What a creature! he thought. He shielded his eyes with his hand and looked up and down the boardwalk.

—I am going to get some breakfast for us. I will be back in a minute.

—Then we will meet over there, said Mora, pointing to a place on the beach. Let us agree to say when you return with our breakfast that you have been gone a month. This month to come will be my secret month, one of the two months that Eila Amblin slept. For even a girl without a memory should have secrets that she knows. She of all people for whom everything is a secret.

—But how will you live for a month? asked 1890
Selah.

He felt the hot morning sun on his face, and it was good. He could feel the circumstances all around him easing. And before him, this tricksome, winsome girl.

—A month is not so long when it is morning time, she said. Go get breakfast, and I will sit here looking out to sea like a widow whose sailor husband died in a storm long ago, although she is still young.

—Grand, said Selah. That is just what I was thinking it would be like.

He handed her the pamphlet, *WF 7 J 1978,* which he had in his pocket.

1895 —Here is something to read, he said. I haven't finished it yet. Mostly there are just schematics, no writing.

Mora was still wearing the dress that she had worn when the car had struck her, when he had first seen her standing staring up at the apartment. It was a fine affair, and left her shoulders bare. This drew him to her like a magnet. He kissed her again.

—Good-bye, she said. One month, don't forget. And maybe buy one of those parasols while you're at it.

She ran down a short stair to the sand. Away across the sand she went and sat upon the beach, staring out to sea.

One month, thought Selah to himself, and walked off down the boardwalk.

1900 Mora looked after him as he went, a serious young man in a gray-blue suit walking along the wooden planks as quietly as he could.

She found a good spot and sat down. It was slightly different from the spot she had chosen from far away. She wondered if Selah would notice. Probably he would. The sand was very fine and smooth and even. She moved her finger across the surface and made a little drawing like this:

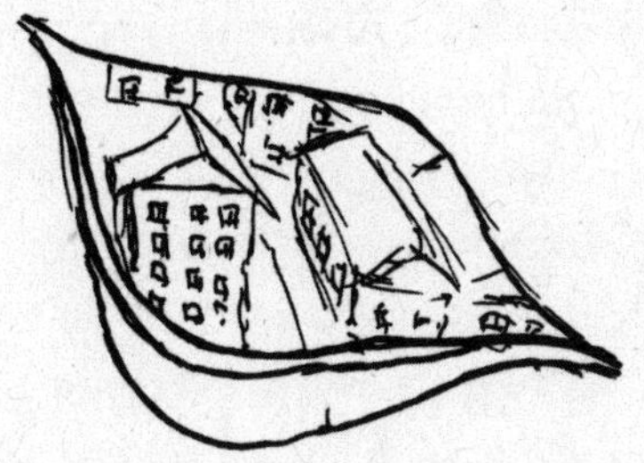

Then she swept the sand away and drew the drawing again. It was exactly the same. Staggeringly so.

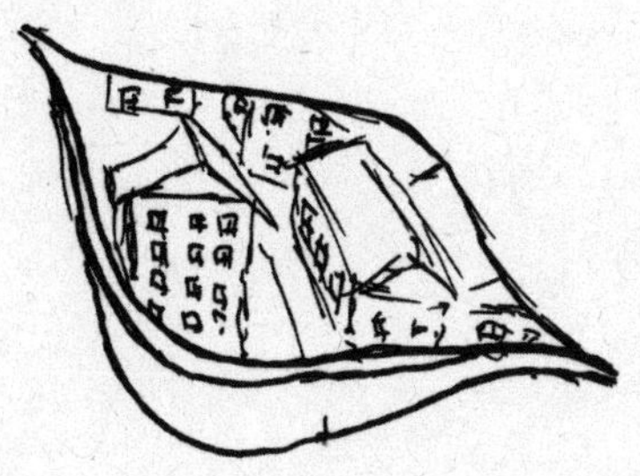

Mora smiled to herself and looked back over her shoulder. Selah was farther down the boardwalk now, standing at a booth, talking to someone. Who was he talking to? She couldn't see the person's face; it was too far away. Selah was holding a parasol and swinging it in a slow circle. She felt certain of him.

—He was right about me, she said to herself.

1905 Her hand moved then rapidly over the sand, drawing her sigil again and again and again. All around her the sand and the boardwalk and the beach drew close up around her, then Coney Island crept, and beyond it on one side New York, on the other the vast Atlantic. The vicinity of Mora Klein became crowded, as though it were a recital being held in a small room when the piano takes up all of the space, but everyone nonetheless refuses to be kept away. Yes, everyone hurried away from what they were doing elsewhere to come here where a girl was sitting and drawing with the tips of her fingers. Everyone came to stand near, and each one held his breath to see what would happen next.

Pau, Jul. 2005

Thanks To

The well situated L'Aragon of Pau, France, where this book was written.

Dimitri Dover, composer of the Devil's fiddle piece.

Gerry Riemer.

Jenny Jackson.

Billy Kingsland.

Martin Carthy (for the folk song, "Geordie").